biscotti and brutality

Snow Falls Alaska Cozy

Book Four

wendy meadows

Majestic Owl Publishing LLC
P.O. Box 997
Newport, NH 03773

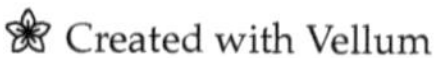

chapter one

Murder.

Bethany Lights could not, for the life of her, understand how she had become directly involved in three murder cases within a year. The first murder case involved a group of killers who trapped her in Snow Falls. The second murder case became a tangled mess at a deserted ski lodge sitting on top of an icy mountain. The third murder case happened in a sleepy lake resort town that rolled up its sidewalks as soon as the sun set. Three murder cases...one year. What were the chances? She didn't know. But Bethany sure wondered if she was cursed. Maybe? Maybe not? The fact was, murder seemed to always be creeping about in her shadow.

Well, at least this morning has been peaceful. To be honest, ever since Julie and I have returned from North Carolina, life hasn't been that horrible. We both witnessed—shockingly—a very pleasant spring and summer. Nothing awful happened. Maybe the three murder cases I survived were the whole shebang, as the saying goes. Bethany listened to her thoughts wander around a cautious mind as she pushed a green shopping cart down a cozy aisle lined with autumn sweaters. *Autumn in Alaska...chimney smoke...brightly colored leaves...pumpkins...corn mazes...hayrides...well, those delightful dreams are the norm. Up here in Alaska, autumn comes early, it seems. In Snow Falls, there aren't any corn mazes or hayrides. Sure, pumpkins are hauled in, and the downtown area is decorated with smiling turkeys and hay bales, but autumn in Alaska isn't like autumn in North Carolina. Still, it's very pleasant...different...kind of lonely...but pleasant.*

Sarah Spencer spotted a lovely woman who was the spitting image of Jane Wyatt from the television show *Father Knows Best*. Sarah couldn't get over how much Bethany resembled Jane Wyatt. "Bethany belongs back in the 1950s, and so do I," Sarah whispered as she watched Bethany examine a green and brown sweater marked twenty percent off. Bethany was wearing a green sweater with brown leaves on it. It was clear the woman was lost in her thoughts and not paying attention to any sweater. Sarah quickly brushed at the jeans she was wearing and carefully approached her friend. "I like that sweater."

"Huh?" Bethany raised her eyes as if a killer was running at her. When she spotted a beautiful, brilliant woman approaching, she formed a quick smile. "Oh, hello, Sarah. Amanda told me you were staying home today."

"Oh, I was." Sarah offered a smile that clearly told Bethany that leaving Amanda alone at O'Mally's meant certain disaster for the snack café. "We have a shipment arriving in about an hour. Amanda turned the slight headache I had into a medical emergency and insisted I stay home. I took some aspirin." Sarah studied Bethany's face as she talked. "The store's been open for about an hour. You're an early shopper. Uh...mind if I intrude and ask if anything is the matter?"

Bethany glanced down at the sweater she was holding. Ever since Bethany had returned from North Carolina with Julie, she had been spending her time cooped up in the coffee shop. Even during the spring and summer months, she dared not venture far from town or her cabin. As for Julie, she took a few nature walks with Amanda and her husband, but that was about as far as she traveled from town. Bethany simply felt afraid to leave Snow Falls. Fear was causing her to feel trapped in a world that became redundant and, sadly, somewhat boring. "Oh. No..."

Sarah slowly folded her arms. "Bethany, when you got back to Snow Falls from North Carolina, you began a routine." She paused. She didn't want Bethany to feel uncomfortable or as if she was about to receive a severe scolding. Sarah knew to proceed using extreme caution. "You open your coffee shop three days a week for five hours, from eight to one. On the days your coffee shop is closed, you spend exactly five hours walking around O'Mally's. When you're not in town, you're at your cabin."

"I suppose I have become a creature of habit," Bethany confessed.

"There's safety and comfort in that. You know your routine, you learn your routine...which means nothing can sneak up on you." Sarah finished her sentence with a sigh.

What could Bethany say? Sarah was right. She had created a routine that offered safety and comforted a nervous woman who had become afraid to even go outside her cabin at night. *I always carry my gun in an ankle holster I bought. I've become scared. Yes. Julie and I survived North Carolina...but so many died. The entire case was filled with one confusing maze after another. I can handle that truth. What I can't handle are the shadows that seem to follow me.*

"Well, perhaps I'm simply content. I've settled down into my new life here in Snow Falls, Sarah...and for once, life has been peaceful."

"Well, yes." Sarah nodded. "The spring and summer months went by with no trouble. At least externally. But in here"—Sarah reached out and gently touched Bethany's heart—"I think there has been a great deal of fear lurking about." Before Bethany could respond, Sarah pushed forward.

"Bethany, when I faced off against the Back Alley Killer, I realized I'd slapped a murderous, evil, soulless monster across the face. And to make matters worse, the Back Alley Killer manipulated my ex-husband...who is dead now...to betray me."

"But I had many long talks with Amanda, Conrad, and Andrew at the coffee shop. They informed me—"

"My family is determined to make everyone believe I'm some kind of Joan of Arc," Sarah cut Bethany off with a gentle smile. "Bethany, I'm retired and living in Alaska running a department store. At least, that's the image I see for myself. But in here"—Sarah touched her own heart this time—"there's always a snarling snowman wearing a leather jacket and chewing on a candy cane...waiting...hiding. Sometimes at night, I wake up in a cold sweat. Sometimes I wake up and see that awful snowman standing at the foot of my bed. Why? Because the fear is always present."

"Yes, I think you're right." Bethany put down the sweater she was holding and looked around. Sarah and Amanda had transformed the inside of O'Mally's into an autumn wonderland. *O'Mally's is safe. I feel secure inside this store. I don't feel afraid.* "I can't stay hidden inside of O'Mally's forever, can I?"

"Afraid not," Sarah informed Bethany. "Right now, my twins are at my cabin being watched by my husband, who'd better do the dishes for once." She shook her head. "Conrad can clean a toilet, but he can't wash a simple breakfast plate. Well, anyway, my point is, every morning when I leave my kids and husband, I do so knowing that anything could happen. There are countless hidden shadows hiding in the snow, Bethany. But I refuse to live my life in fear."

"Sarah, you and Amanda...you were both nearly killed so many times."

"That's true," Sarah said gently. "When Amanda and I became infected with a deadly virus, I thought that was it for us. Light's out, the end. Amanda and I still have to have our blood tested every six months. Dr. Whitfield insists that the blood tests are for precaution only, but sometimes I wonder if he believes the virus will manifest itself again." Sarah shook her head. "Bethany, can you believe a mean grizzly bear helped save me and Amanda? Well, a mean grizzly bear, and some very hot water."

"Yes, Amanda told me about the grizzly bear."

A comforting smile touched Sarah's eyes. "I can live in fear, honey, but even when the monsters think they have me backed into a corner...well, I would have never expected a grizzly bear to come to my rescue." She motioned around O'Mally's. "I love this old store more than I can put into words, but sometimes Conrad and I take the kids away. Take this summer, for instance. Conrad and I took the twins to see Pete. We had a fun time filled with lots of laughs. Could something bad have happened? Sure. Something bad can happen just getting out of bed."

"Are you suggesting I take a trip?" Bethany asked in a nervous voice. "Sarah, I don't think I'm ready."

"I'm suggesting you and Julie sit down and talk," Sarah said with a big-sister tone. "Julie has the same look in her eyes as you do." She reached her right hand into the front pocket of her jeans. Bethany made a curious face, and Sarah smiled. "Here," she told Bethany, bringing out a green brochure. "Look at this."

Bethany accepted the brochure with an uneasy hand. "Autumn in Vermont?" she asked.

Sarah nodded. "There's a town in Vermont called Hay Lake. It's a small town situated close to the Canadian border. A friend of mine—well, two friends—own a bed and breakfast in Hay Lake." Sarah tapped the brochure. "Hay Lake is known for fun hayrides, pumpkin fields, corn mazes, and an amazing Pumpkin Festival. In the winter, Hay Lake has a wonderful Winter Festival."

Bethany opened the brochure Sarah had handed her. Her eyes drank in pictures of cozy pumpkin fields filled with hay wagons and smiling families. Dazzling, breathtaking autumn trees lined the edges of the pumpkin fields. The scene was very welcoming and inviting. "This brochure is nice, Sarah, but I don't think I'm ready to take a trip."

"My friends Jim and Jill Cunningham are wonderful people, Bethany. Jim and Jill are in their mid-sixties, and they're both retired comedians. Just imagine the laughs." Sarah smiled. "Jim is a brilliant pianist. He was inspired to go into comedy after seeing a live performance by Victor Borge when he was a younger man. Jill was a schoolteacher and used her comedy to inspire students to learn. When she met Jim, they hit the road together."

"I'm sure they're both very nice." Bethany nodded. Sarah was gently pressing Bethany to leave Snow Falls, but it was clear Bethany wasn't ready to part with her comfort zone.

"They are," Sarah smiled. "Anyway, I called my friends and told them about you and Julie. They agreed to keep two rooms open for the next month, just in case you and Julie take a trip. And who knows?" Sarah gently nudged Bethany with her shoulder. "You two might meet your Mr. Rights? You don't have to stay single forever if you don't want to. Somewhere out there, Bethany, the right man is waiting."

Bethany felt her cheeks turn red. Romance was alien to her heart. "Oh, maybe someday. I'm content in knowing I'm free from a horrible marriage." She spoke without lifting her eyes from the brochure Sarah had handed her. *The scenes are pleasant and welcoming, and Vermont is beautiful in the autumn. I can almost smell the hay...the bonfires...the apple cider...the pumpkin pies. It would be nice to take a trip away from Snow Falls. As much as I love and adore my new home, I admit I have allowed myself to become caged in. And maybe Sarah is right? I can't stay locked inside of O'Mally's for the rest of my life. Sooner or later, I will have to venture out into the world again or go crazy. I mean, there's only so many green sweaters a woman can buy. But what if I take a trip to relax but end up being chased by monsters again?*

"Honey."

"Huh?" Bethany lifted her eyes. Sarah was staring at her in a way that told Bethany the woman was reading her troubled thoughts like an open book.

"I can't force you to take a trip, but I can promise you one thing," Sarah spoke in a voice that became very serious. "If you allow yourself to live in constant fear, you will never escape the shadows. As scared as your heart can become—especially for a woman—there comes a time when you must open a locked door and step back into the world."

"Sarah—"

"Bethany, you're a fighter," Sarah continued. "I see an amazing strength in you, and an amazing intelligence—an intelligence I would even consider dangerous, to be honest. You should have been a cop." Bethany shook her head modestly and let out a nervous laugh. Sarah simply smiled. "Bethany, you're becoming a new woman...let that new woman breathe and have life. And if that means you continue getting dragged into a cage filled with monsters, so be it. I would much rather fight to my death than cower in a corner hiding from every shadow."

Before Bethany could answer, a nervous girl named Rachel ran up to Sarah. "Uh...Sarah, the food truck is here, and Amanda is already taking stock of how many kosher hot dogs there are," the girl said urgently.

"Oh no, Amanda." Sarah quickly patted Bethany's hand. "Honey, I'm always here for you. You're my family now. Think about what we talked about. In the meantime, I have to stop Amanda from eating all the kosher dogs."

Bethany watched Sarah take off at a full sprint. As she did, a curious thought struck her troubled heart. *Sarah and Amanda were nearly killed on many occasions, yet look at them. Every day, they embrace life.* Bethany dropped her eyes back down to the brochure she was holding. *No one knows Sarah gave me this brochure. Maybe I can take a fun trip...but not alone.* Bethany lowered the brochure, then she reached into a white purse, retrieved a cell phone, and called Julie. "Julie, are you busy?"

"I'm sitting here eating ice cream and watching reruns," Julie admitted in a bored voice.

"Uh, want a change of scenery?" Bethany asked, drawing in a few deep, brave breaths. "And maybe a few laughs?"

chapter two

"Oh, look at the lake!" Julie exclaimed, speaking in a thick British accent that caused Ron Taylor to smile. Ron Taylor was a seventy-eight-year-old man who drove the only cab in Hay Lake—"cab" being a generous word for a 1968 Chevrolet Impala that was rusted down to the core and rattled so badly that the wheels nearly wobbled off. No matter. Ron loved his old car. Lots of memories…wonderful memories.

Bethany spotted a sun-glittered lake between a line of thick, lush autumn trees. The little back road Ron was traveling down wrapped around the back side of Hay Lake, allowing Bethany and Julie a look at the countryside. On the west side of the lake stood the small town of Hay Lake—cozy hotels, stores, restaurants, and other small-town features lined the front of the lake. Orange Lead Road stretched through Hay Lake and took people to various farms, pumpkin patches, campgrounds, and a lovely fairground. The east side of the lake—or the backside, as Ron insisted—was for the people who called Hay Lake home. Miles and miles of cozy back roads splintered away from the lake, leading to beautiful homes.

Jim and Jill Cunningham lived north of the lake on Winter

Dove Road. Winter Dove Road connected to the little back road that ran along the back side of the lake. Bethany subconsciously made mental notes of the layout and directions. *Relax. Nothing bad has happened. The flight to Vermont went off without a problem. No luggage was lost, no planes crashed, no murderers appeared. You're in Hay Lake with your best friend.* "It is beautiful."

Ron glanced in the old rearview mirror and spotted two lovely women sitting in the back seat of his car. Bethany's red hair was very striking—and lovely. Bethany reminded him of an old actress he knew but couldn't name. Julie, Ron thought, looked like a dazzling British beauty with dark black hair. Julie reminded Ron of his own wife, who had died of cancer five years prior. Of course, Ron's wife had not been British, but it was interesting how Julie resembled her. "Going to be cold tonight. Temperatures will drop into the low thirties. Hope you two brought a sweater." Ron pronounced the word "sweater" as "sweatah." The old man spoke with a heavy Brooklyn accent.

"Oh, we did," Bethany assured Ron. "My friend and I live in, uh, Alaska." *Why didn't I say the name of the town? I have to stop being so nervous.* "We're used to the cold."

"I should say so," Julie added and let out a quick laugh. Like Bethany, she felt nervous being so far away from home. But also like Bethany, it was time to venture back out into the world again. "Cousin Amanda had a long talk with me," she told Bethany. "I know I already told you what we talked about, but I can't stop hearing what Amanda's last words were before we ended our talk."

"'Fear takes away the joy of eating a chili kosher hot dog dripping with cheese,'" Bethany said, smiling some.

"Yes." Julie rolled her eyes. "My cousin has a way of making a woman realize that she can't stay locked away in her bedroom for life." She flicked her eyes toward a beautiful lake peeking through the beautiful autumn trees. "When you suggested we take this trip, I was shocked...and relieved. Anyway, love, I'm determined to spend the next seven days having a wonderful time. And you know what?"

"What?" Bethany asked.

"I feel I can breathe a little better now that I've left my comfort zone," Julie confessed. "Snow Falls isn't going anywhere. We can enjoy ourselves."

Bethany watched Julie fold her arms, which were covered by a lovely blue and white sweater draped over khaki cargo pants. Julie was tense, but the woman was clearly determined to stop living in fear.

I am uneasy, but if I let the shadows consume me, I'll never be free. I refuse to be scared. Sarah leaves her house every day knowing that the snowman could show up. My own snowman can show up at any time, but I have to stop living in fear. Bethany locked her eyes on a line of dazzling autumn trees, and for a minute, she felt her heart actually...relax. *I may be crazy, but I'm feeling very glad I took this trip.*

"It's still early. Maybe after we get checked in, we can go into town and wander around some of the antique shops?"

"Oh, that sounds fun," Julie beamed. "But first, maybe we can eat? I'm starving."

"Uh...we ate at the airport," Bethany teased Julie a little.

"Well, Amanda's blood runs in me." Julie laughed. "The four breakfast biscuits I ate didn't fill my tummy."

Bethany laughed. It felt good to laugh. "I guess not."

Ron smiled and tittered down a sleepy back road, eventually arriving at a large two-story home sitting at the end of a long driveway lined with bright autumn trees. "Oh my." Bethany and Julie both gasped as Ron drove up the driveway. Lines of breathtaking rolling hills filled their eyes. The hills were soaked with autumn leaves and complemented by two old barns, a lovely duck pond, and a cozy pumpkin patch. Off to the right side of the main house, countless milk cows were out grazing.

"Jim and Jill own a nice place. Used to be a real dump out here until they fixed it up," Ron explained, easing his car through a small covered bridge that ran over a sleepy stream. The bridge creaked and groaned but held.

"Well, here we are." Ron pulled his car up next to a green truck that was winter tough. "I'll get your luggage."

"How much do we owe you?" Bethany asked.

"Well, the drive up from the capital ain't like driving down the road to get some milk," Ron informed Bethany. "I got to pay for my gas...so how about...a hundred dollars?" Ron turned an old, street-worn face around and adjusted a ball cap he was wearing. "Fifty bucks apiece sound about right?"

"Sure does." Bethany quickly grabbed her purse before Julie could react. She snatched out twenty-dollar bills and counted. "Here." She handed Ron one hundred and forty dollars. "I added a tip." *And why not? This old man drove out of his way to pick me and Julie up. And he's so nice.*

"You're okay." Ron smiled at Bethany as he took his money. "You ladies go on inside and I'll get your luggage."

Julie smiled. "Come on, love." With those words, she climbed out into a crisp, delightful, autumn morning and stretched her arms. "Oh, smell the chimney smoke in the air...and look at the milk cows."

Bethany crawled out of Ron's car and looked around. *This land is so beautiful,* she thought, feeling a gentle wind brush the green sweater she was wearing—a green sweater she had bought at O'Mally's. *If I were back home, I would be at O'Mally's right now looking at the same old sweaters. It's time to take a deep breath and relax.* "I love milk cows."

Before Julie could respond, a heavy wooden door attached to the brown two-story house swung open. A tall, skinny, gray-headed woman quickly appeared.

"Hey, Jim," Jill Cunningham called out in an irritated voice, "Ron done brought us more of them tourists. You better get the chainsaw!" She deliberately spoke in a heavy Texan tone even though she was a Yankee.

A short, plump man who immediately reminded Bethany of the dad from the television series *Happy Days* appeared beside his wife (the plump man even had the last name—oh, the irony). He covered his eyes with a quick hand and studied the scene. "Nah, we better use the ax on them. Chainsaw is rusty," Jim said, transforming a heavy Georgia accent into a hard Canadian voice. "I sharpened the ax last night."

Ron rolled his eyes. "And you two wonder why you get no business?" he called out.

"Basement is too full of bodies. Told you to stop bringing us these tourists until we could get rid of the bodies, Ron!" Jim fussed, and pointed at Bethany and Julie. "You two like finger soup? Maybe me and the wife can fatten you up for the slaughter?"

Bethany and Julie glanced at each other and then looked back at Jim and Jill. Jill was wearing a brown sweater with the words "I'm with this Moron" printed on it along with an arrow that pointed at Jim. Jim was wearing an orange sweater with the words "I'm with this Old Bat" printed on it along with a hard finger pointing at his wife. "Maybe we better get checked in before you kill us?" Bethany suggested.

Jill tossed her eyes at Jim. "What do you think?" she asked.

Jim's face twisted into a curious expression. "Might as well. Sheriff Nayes has been snooping around. Best if we kill them after the sun sets." Jim grinned a hideous smile. "Come inside, ladies," he called out, turning his voice into that of a creepy undertaker and eased back into a warm, cozy foyer as if he were a monster.

"They're insane," Ron warned Bethany and Julie. "The older they get, the more their minds go." He rolled his eyes again and looked toward the house. "Jill," he called out, "saw

Mac driving toward town. Been meaning to ask how Paula is doing. Any word?"

Jill smiled. She loved acting crazy. "Ron, you know as well as I do that Paula Towers is the biggest hypochondriac in Hay Lake. Now stop gabbing and get the luggage inside. And you two"—Jill pointed at Bethany and Julie—"here are the rules: no loud music, no drugs, no smoking, no drinking, no parties...those are the serious rules! Now, here are the not-so-serious rules: no breathing, no talking, no eating, no moving...understand? But be sure to pay me first before you follow the rules—cash only—ten grand a night! And for goodness' sake, if the mafia shows up, just duck and cover!" With those words, Jill tipped Ron. "Oh, one last rule: all guests have to milk the cows."

"And slaughter the chickens!" Jim yelled from inside the house.

Ron let out a chuckle. "Last people who stayed here lasted two hours. Best wishes, ladies."

Bethany glanced at Julie. To her relief, Julie was smiling. "I'll slaughter the chickens only if you cook them!" Julie called back to Jim.

"Deal!"

"Hey, Jim, I like her! Maybe we'll keep her alive," Jill told her husband. She hurried off the lovely front porch filled with rocking chairs and approached Bethany and Julie. Smiling, she said, "With all kidding aside, welcome to Hay Lake. Sarah Garland—uh, Spencer—told me and that man inside I call a husband so much about you. Whoever is a friend of Sarah's is a friend of ours." She quickly shook Bethany's and Julie's hands. "Now, let's get you two settled and then we'll drive into town and have a pleasant lunch."

"That sounds lovely," Julie beamed. "I love antique shops. And I'm starving, too."

"My friend loves antique shops, and she is starving." Bethany smiled, and then drew in a deep breath of crisp air that smelled of autumn chimney smoke, pumpkins...and cow manure. "You have a lovely home, and the land is breathtaking."

"This land was neglected for a long time," Jill explained. "Jim and I invested every penny we had into this land and the house. We've been here for—"

"Ten years," Ron called out as he popped open a rusted trunk that smelled of oil and gas.

Jill smiled. "Jim and I used to live in Los Angeles. That's where we met Sarah. Anyway, we can talk later. Let's get you two checked in."

Jim came hurrying out of the house before Bethany or Julie could say a word. He rushed down to his wife and grabbed her arm. "Uh, inside, now. It's bad...terrible...oh my..." Jim ran his wife back inside.

"Come on," Ron fussed, grabbing two green suitcases. "Let's get inside and see what prank they're up to. Knowing those two, whatever it is, it'll be crazy."

"Come on, love." Julie patted Bethany's arm and trudged after Ron. "Let's go investigate. It might be fun."

Bethany stood still a minute instead of following Julie. *This land is beautiful...and peaceful. Soon the snow will arrive, and the land will be covered in white. Hot chocolate...sleigh rides...Christmas lights...it'll be so beautiful. Snow Falls is beautiful during the winter...the snow is home. And the people of Snow Falls go to great lengths to make the town look cozy and lovely for Christmas. But there always seems to be something missing. Or maybe something is missing inside of me?*

A lazy milk cow lifted its head, looked toward Bethany for a few seconds, and went back to chewing on some brown grass. A powerful gust of wind picked up a pile of leaves and scattered them over the cow's head. The cow didn't have a care in the world. *Any second, someone could appear and attack that cow, but that cow doesn't care. Life must move forward, and that cow knows it.* As Bethany stared at the milk cow, her mind replayed the words Sarah had spoken to her weeks before inside O'Mally's. *I can't live in fear because if I do, the shadows will win. That silly milk cow is surrounded by a dangerous world, but she's brave enough to stand out in the open and enjoy a beautiful day.* A strange anger touched Bethany's heart at that moment. *How dare anyone try to make me live in fear? I may live and be free. I will not be scared anymore. If there's shadows waiting for me, so be it. I will not remain imprisoned. Now, it's time to enjoy my vacation. I will not stay caged up. I will enjoy my vacation, even if it kills me.*

Bethany drew in a deep, brave breath and started up toward the house. As she did, a horrible scream burst out through the front door. The scream, Bethany realized, was the relative of a corny prank. Bethany could handle Jim's and Jill's humor. "Oh, brother."

The sound of an approaching vehicle caught Bethany's attention. She turned around and spotted an old Ford Bronco that had been converted into a sheriff's vehicle.

Sheriff Ben Nayes was on his way to Jim's and Jill's place to deliver some very interesting news. Murder was back in the air.

chapter three

Sheriff Ben Nayes spotted a lovely woman standing beside old Ron's rusted car—a car that should have been hauled off to a junkyard years ago. He carefully parked beside Jim's and Jill's truck, checked a brown sheriff's uniform that needed some tending to, rubbed his hand over a rough, thin beard, and stepped out into the refreshing autumn wind. "Hello," he called out to Bethany.

Bethany looked at a ruggedly handsome man who appeared to be her age. "Hello," she answered politely.

"I'm Sheriff Ben Nayes. People around here just call me Ben." Ben glanced around. Jim and Jill were probably inside. If old Ron's junker was parked in the driveway, that meant guests were on the scene. The beautiful woman standing beside Ron's car was probably a guest. "Is Jim and Jill Cunningham—"

"Murder!" Jill burst out through the front door screaming her lungs out. "They done killed! Oh, it's horrible!"

Jim ran out after Jill. "Sheriff Nayes, inside. Hurry!" he screamed in a voice that sounded very convincing. "It's blood...everywhere..."

Ben only smiled. "I see you two are practicing. Good," he told Jim and Jill. "I've come to tell you that you've been approved to turn your bed and breakfast into a murder house. Thought I'd bring you the news myself. County commissioners were really against the issue. The idea of a murder house didn't sit well with many people. I was surprised I didn't see you two at the meeting last night."

"You know I can't stand those snotty commissioners." Jim quickly wiped a pair of hands covered with fake blood on his trousers. "Jill and I assumed our request would be shot down, so we didn't waste our time."

"Well, to be honest, if I hadn't spoken up..." Ben glanced toward Bethany before continuing. "Jim, you and Jill want to have an innocent, fun, murder house—"

"Murder Mystery House," Jill corrected Ben. She turned to Jim and wiped a pair of red hands on his shirt.

"Murder Mystery House." Ben nodded. "Well, it didn't seem right to me for our elected officials to be putting up such a fuss simply because they're still sore you have ownership of this land. I also reminded them we live in a free republic and if they denied your request, well, lawsuits might follow because there is plenty of proof that the commissioners have been biased against you in the past. And because we live in a world consumed by social media outlets—and you both know how poisonous I think all social media is—I reminded our elected officials it wouldn't be difficult to throw gas onto a small fire, a fire that would burn them. I also reminded our elected officials that just last month they approved a liquor license request to a shabby pool hall that sits on the outskirts of town while denying you the right to sell raw milk on your land. With elections coming up, and with the races being so close, I think our officials got the point I was trying to convey."

"Thanks, Ben." Jim quickly walked over to Ben and shook the man's hand. "You've always been a good friend. You're the only man who has any guts in this county."

"Hopefully some good people will get voted in," Ben told

Jim. "The five commissioners we have now believe they are set in stone. It's time to get the bad out and the good in. Hay Lake is suffering because of a few bad weeds."

"The bad news is that most of the people who live in Hay Lake are seasonal. The full-timers are the only ones who vote, and they vote for the same old names because that's all they know." Jim shook his head. "When winter hits, Hay Lake thins out like a fat buffalo herd being chased by a hungry group of women who have been on Weight Watchers for too long."

"Hey, I was on Weight Watchers," said Jill. "And you're not exactly Mr. Slim Jim, Fatso."

"Fatso...well." Jim rubbed his plump belly. "Maybe I do like pumpkin pie a bit too much." He chuckled.

"I'd say you're married to your fat rolls." Jill walked over to her husband and elbowed his tubby belly. "The stairs are complaining, Jim, and the milk cows are getting jealous."

Jim chuckled again. He loved Jill's sense of humor, even though it was rough at his expense. "Well, Old Betsy can stay jealous." He focused on Ben. "Why don't you come in for a cup of coffee and a slice of, uh, pumpkin pie?"

"Sounds good." Ben glanced at Bethany.

"Oh, Ben, meet Ms. Bethany Lights. She's visiting us all the way from Snow Falls, Alaska," Jill quickly blurted out. "Bethany is Sarah Garland—uh, Spencer's—friend. I keep forgetting that Sarah married that cop from New York."

Ben was aware of who Sarah was. Sarah was the famous detective who took down the Back Alley Killer with help from Amanda Hardcastle. "You're a long way from home, Ms. Lights. Sometimes I wonder how people end up here in Hay Lake?"

"Sarah suggested I visit," Bethany answered, keeping her voice polite. "I'm visiting with a friend, Julie Walsh."

"Julie is British," Jill cut in. "Pretty as a button, too." She quickly scooted over to Bethany. "Ben is currently single...hint, hint."

A loud moan left Ben's mouth. "Jill, if you don't beat everything."

Jim laughed. "My wife isn't very subtle, Ben, you know that. She's been trying to marry you off for the last five years."

"Ever since you finally wised up and divorced that spider you were married to," Jill added.

Ben quickly rubbed the back of his neck. "Ms. Lights," he spoke directly to Bethany, "I was married...been divorced for the last five years. And as you can see, Jill Cunningham is determined to marry me off again. So far she's tried to set me up on about a thousand blind dates."

"Well, why not?" Jill threw her hands up into the air. "You're a handsome man, Ben. A man like you shouldn't be alone. What are you, Sheriff Andy Taylor raising Opie or something? You don't even have a kid, for crying out loud!"

"I have Aunt Bee," Ben teased.

Jill walked over to Ben and kicked him in the leg. "Nola Rogers is a horrible woman. Never mention her name!"

Jim laughed again. "My wife was sore that Nola Rogers took the blue ribbon for best apple pie."

"I'd say she is still sore," Ben moaned in pain.

"Nola Rogers cheats somehow!" Jill snapped her arms together. "Someday, I will prove that woman has been cheating all these years and you will arrest her."

"I can't arrest my aunt, Jill." Ben rubbed his leg. "Jim, how about that coffee, huh?"

Before anyone could move or say another word, a fancy gray Ford truck came speeding up the driveway. Jim placed a hand over his eyes, studied the truck, and shook his head. "Richard Banks is paying us a visit."

Jill stepped close to her husband. "Trouble is brewing, Pa. We best get the cows in." She spoke in a voice meant to sound silly, but there was a hint of concern.

"Let me handle Richard," Ben cautioned. "Ms. Lights, you better get inside."

"No, we might need a witness," Jim warned.

Before Ben could object, the fancy Ford truck slid to a stop, causing a small dust cloud, and a tall, scrawny, angry man wearing an expensive gray suit jumped out like a wet hornet. "I was told you were here, Ben! How dare you threaten my wife!" Richard Banks stormed up to Ben, throwing a boney finger in the air. "I knew I should have attended the meeting last night! I thought it was an open-and-shut matter! You had no right to interfere!"

Ben narrowed his eyes as Bethany tensed. "Lower your finger," he warned Richard.

"You're a tough guy, huh?" Richard snapped, speaking in a thick Boston accent. "You don't scare me. The only reason you're sheriff is because you—"

"Because people respect me," Ben answered in a fierce growl. "Richard, you're trespassing on private property. Leave."

"This was my land!" Richard yelled at Ben. "Those two jokers stole this land from me and you know it!"

"This was never your land, Richard. The land went up for auction and Mr. and Mrs. Cunningham bought this land fair and square." Ben stepped in front of Jim and Jill protectively. "Now I told you to leave."

"I'll get my land!" Richard yelled at Jim and Jill. "You wait and see...and your little idea to turn your stupid bed and breakfast into some freak show won't save you. I know you're hurting for money!"

"I said leave!" Ben snapped in a tone that caused Richard to step back. "This land will stay in possession of Jim and Jill Cunningham. Is that clear, Richard? Even if I have to dip into my own savings to help them keep this land, I will. But I assure you, my friends are not hurting for money."

"That's right," Jim stepped past Ben. "You may work at

the bank, Mr. Banks, and that's why my wife and I don't keep our money at the bank. We keep our money in a private bank."

"But we keep a little money in the local bank—fool's money." Jill stepped up next to her husband. "How would you know we're hurting for money unless you've been peeking at our private financial records, huh? You lousy dog? Somebody needs to neuter you! Jim, go get my hedge trimmers!"

"Richard, you better leave," Ben warned. "I may not be able to hold my friends back for much longer."

"Oh, you think this is funny!" Richard raised a hard finger at Ben. "Your days are numbered, and so are their—"

A loud gunshot penetrated the air before Richard could finish his sentence. Bethany heard the gunshot and saw Richard Banks fly backward, crash up against the driver's side door of his truck, and splatter down onto the ground like a fried egg.

"Down!" Ben yelled. He grabbed Jim and Jill and yanked them down onto the ground. Bethany followed. Ben pulled out the Beretta 92X Performance he had resting in his gun holster and eyed Richard's body. Somebody had put a bullet in the man's chest. Ben glanced back toward the house. The bullet had come from that direction.

"Who is in the house?"

"Just Ron and Julie Walsh," Jill answered quickly. "Jim's hunting rifles are upstairs, locked in his hunting case."

"That's right," Jim confirmed calmly. Unknown to Bethany, Jim had served in the Marines as a young man. He wasn't the type of man to fall apart or lose control when a situation turned hairy. He nodded toward Richard. "Ben, he's dead. I can tell by the way he's laying."

Ben eyed the house. "Gunshot came from the house—"

"Not in the house, far right side," Jim corrected Ben. "Near the wood pile."

This can't be happening. Bethany could barely believe her eyes. Had a man really been shot dead? Was some sick prank being played? Was the scene part of Jim's and Jill's Murder Mystery House? Bethany didn't know. What she knew was that there was a pool of red blood around Richard Banks's chest. *That man is dead. I can look at him and clearly see he's dead. This isn't a prank. But how can this be? Did a shadow—did the snowman Sarah fears—follow me from Snow Falls? Is the same snowman now haunting me?*

Ben glanced toward the far right side of the house. He spotted no one near a tall wood pile that rested against the side of it. "Stay here." Ben quickly crawled military style over to Richard Banks and checked the man for any signs of life. "He's dead, Jim," he called back over his shoulder. "Listen to me, whoever killed Richard could have taken a shot at any of us. Take Jill and get inside. Ms. Lights, you get inside, too. I'm calling this in."

"Let's go!" Jim ordered Jill and Bethany. "On your feet. Move!"

Bethany felt instinct take over. She scrambled to her legs and ran into a safe, warm, secure house with Jim and Jill as Ben crawled to his car and called in for backup. "We heard the gunshot," Ron's voice greeted Bethany as soon as she dashed into a small foyer that was decorated with lovely autumn leaves. Julie was bent down beside Ron. "Is Richard Banks dead? Did someone finally kill that worm?"

"Looks that way." Jim knelt beside Ron and looked outside. He watched Ben call in the scene and look around before running up onto the front porch and making his way inside. "What now, Ben?"

Ben caught sight of Julie Walsh. For a second, he felt his heart stop. Julie was the most beautiful woman he had ever seen. Yes, Bethany was beautiful. But Julie...something about the woman caught Ben's heart. "Uh, I need to check the back. Keep everyone here." He quickly shook his head to regain brain function and darted out of the foyer and down a long hallway that led back to a spacious farm kitchen.

"Love, what happened?" Julie grabbed Bethany's hand. "Are you all right?"

"I'm...fine." Bethany stepped aside as Jim locked the front door. "I was standing outside. I heard a gunshot, and then..." She stopped talking and stared into Julie's eyes. "Julie, I think the snowman followed us from Snow Falls."

"The snowman?" Ron asked. "What in the world are you talking about?"

"You wouldn't understand, Mr. Taylor." Julie sighed miserably. "I was hoping for the best, love."

"Me, too." *Every day when we wake up, we have to accept that we will face the unknown. I can either run or fight. I can't live my life in fear. But my goodness...a man is dead.* For a second, Bethany felt like crumbling, but then she saw Sarah's brave face in her mind. *Sarah never caved in or ran. Yes, Sarah lives with fear every day of her life, but she's a fighter. I have to be a fighter. Sarah wouldn't care about me if she didn't believe I had the ability to fight.* "Julie, maybe the snowman followed us. Maybe the snowman left Sarah alone and attached itself to us? All we can do is fight."

Yes, You can fight, Bethany, but you will never win. Oh, the weather outside is frightening...very frightening. Bethany saw a hideous snowman wearing a leather jacket and chewing a candy cane in her mind before the vision vanished into the snow.

chapter four

The sound of slamming ambulance doors caused Bethany to snap back to reality. An ambulance was parked in the leaf-covered driveway. A middle-aged man with a thick mustache wearing a blue paramedic uniform walked over to Ben, spoke a few words, and made his way into the driver's seat of the ambulance. Bethany waited until the ambulance drove away before she approached Ben. "What now?" she asked carefully.

"John," Ben spoke to a young deputy, who appeared eager to take on a herd of outlaws alone, "go see what's keeping Charlie with the dogs."

John Merrit offered a quick nod and rushed off toward a brown sheriff's deputy car. "He's eager," Bethany spoke before she could help herself.

"Yeah, but he's a good kid." Ben turned to face a concerned pair of eyes. "Charlie Wager should be on the scene with his dogs any minute. We're going to scout the area. I don't want to spook the tourists. Hay Lake depends on tourist to stay alive. I'm going to keep the killing silent. That means—"

"Silence. I understand." Bethany wrapped her arms around her chest and looked around. The land was so beautiful and cozy, like a delicate, warm blanket designed to sooth troubled hearts...at least in Bethany's eyes. Murder had brought an ugly stain to the land. "Sheriff Nayes—"

"Ben."

"Julie and I are checked in. We would like to stay the night." Bethany continued coldly, "We will leave tomorrow morning."

"No need." Ben walked his eyes up onto a sleepy front porch. Julie was standing there with Jim, Jill, and Ron. "Bethany, I'm not shutting down Jim's and Jill's home. They depend on tourists, too. Like I said, I'm going to keep the killing silent. Scarlet Fredrick—she's the mayor of Hay Lake—has agreed. Scarlet clearly understands that without tourists, Hay Lake will suffer a severe financial blow."

Bethany focused back on Ben's face. A deep strain of worry was blistering the man's eyes. "You won't be able to keep the killing a secret and you know it. Why? Because the county commissioner's—"

"Richard's wife will cause a storm. The woman has been notified. She has to go the hospital and identify the body. I've explained to her we need to keep the killing silent. There's no reason to spook the community." Ben studied an autumn-soaked land that should have been filled with laughing children wandering through corn mazes instead of...murder. "Rhonda Banks will be a problem."

This problem is a local matter. Whoever the shooter is specifically targeted Richard Banks. The shooter could have killed anyone. However, I have a bad hunch that Richard Banks's murder will somehow be tied to the Cunninghams. There's more going on behind the scenes than meets the eye. But do I want to become involved? Julie and I can leave right now, or first thing tomorrow morning. Bethany felt very troubled. The killing of Richard Banks, she had concluded, did not involve her or Julie. But could she walk away? Would Sarah walk away? *Maybe Julie and I will stay the night and ask a few questions. Jim and Jill are innocent...eccentric, yes, but good people. They're not killers.* "Well, I'll be inside with Julie if you need us."

"I'll be along shortly. I have to talk to Jim and Jill." Ben glanced toward Julie again. Goodness, Julie sure was a beautiful dream standing on the front porch. Julie caught Ben looking at her, blushed some, and then quickly focused on Jim and Jill.

"Alright." Bethany refused to become personal with anyone. *Julie and I will stay until morning and see what happens. If Jim and Jill Cunningham are in trouble...well, I don't know. I don't want to involve myself, but Jim and Jill are Sarah's friends, and Sarah wouldn't turn a blind eye to this matter. Out of respect for Sarah I'll stay until morning and see what happens.*

Bethany walked back up onto the front porch, made small chit chat for a minute, and then journeyed up to the second floor of a warm house. There, she found a lovely, spacious room that would be her temporary home. "Autumn leaf wallpaper...hardwood floors...old popcorn ceilings...a large bay window overlooking a backyard pond...an old-fashioned bed...old farm furnishings...very picturesque." A deep desire to fall in love with the room overwhelmed Bethany's heart. However, Bethany wasn't in the mood to relax or enjoy the atmosphere. She found her luggage sitting at the foot of the bed, stood still for a moment, and walked over to the bay window, focusing on the quaint little duck pond surrounded by lovely rolling hills. "Sarah, I know Jim and Jill are your friends, and I know you wouldn't turn you back on them, but am I expected to involve myself? Is your snowman chasing me now?"

A hand quickly knocked on the heavy bedroom door. Bethany turned away from the window and answered the visitor with a quick "Come in."

Jill Cunningham opened the door and slipped into Bethany's room.

"Are you getting settled in all right?" Jill asked in a courteous voice.

"I will," Bethany assured Jill. Jill didn't come to see if her guests were getting settled in okay. She had other matters on her mind, and Bethany knew it. "Are you all right? I know this morning has been difficult for you and Jim."

"Oh, I'll shed no tears for Richard Banks," Jill confessed as she closed the bedroom door with her right hand. "Richard Banks had a stink that could make a skunk roll up and whimper. The man was a menace, a constant threat. Now that he's taking a dirt nap—well, forgive me if this sounds hateful, even soulless, but I'll sleep a little easier at night."

"Except for Rhonda Banks, right? Rhonda Banks won't let you rest easy, will she?" Bethany knew she was presenting a sudden hard question that Jill might not be emotionally or mentally prepared to answer, but such questions had to be asked. Bethany knew she didn't have the time to make meaningless small talk. Jill was present for a reason. Bethany needed to uncover that reason and bring hidden truths to light.

"Rhonda Banks is one of the county commissioners. She's a rattlesnake wrapped up in the poison of a scorpion." Jill walked her eyes around Bethany's room. "Bethany, Sarah told me a great deal about you. Sarah emphasized you were a smart lady." She took her eyes back to a concerned face holding intense focus. "Sarah also informed me you have solved three murders within the last year."

"Not willingly," Bethany confessed. *Why would Sarah tell a woman I don't even know about past matters?*

"I bet," Jill nodded. "Murder is ugly business. That's how Sarah and I met in Los Angeles. Jim and I were fostering a sixteen-year-old kid who killed someone. The kid had severe problems...Jim and I thought we could help him. We were wrong. We're blessed that kid killed his drug dealer instead of us."

"Murder is ugly," Bethany agreed.

Jill walked over to an old wooden rocking chair sitting next to a quiet fireplace and sat down. "Bethany, I was a schoolteacher before I went on the road with Jim as a comedian. I admit I was a rough teacher. Public schools are rough places, especially in Los Angeles. My duty was to help society's outcasts have a chance at life. I encountered a lot of hard kids, and many times, I dedicated myself to those kids in ways that became very personal."

"Is that why you fostered a killer?"

Jill nodded. "No one wanted Wayne Tyler. Wayne's case worker was at her wit's end. Wayne had been in and out of countless foster homes before he reached my shore. I wanted to believe there was good in Wayne. I needed to believe there was good in the kid, so I talked Jim into allowing me to foster him. Three weeks later, Wayne killed his drug dealer." Jill let out a heavy sigh. "Wayne killed his drug dealer in some grimy alley. At the same time, Sarah was chasing down the Back Alley Killer. Wayne led Sarah straight to my front door. Sarah arrested a punk kid instead of the Back Alley Killer. And let me tell you, the Back Alley Killer had everyone in Los Angeles shaking in their boots. For a few days, Jim and I wondered if we were fostering the real Back Alley Killer. Thank goodness we were wrong."

"From the research I conducted, I learned that the Back Alley Killer was a vicious killer." Bethany eased over to a brown sitting chair resting close to the rocking chair. She eased down onto the chair and continued. "Jill, are you concerned that Wayne Tyler might be involved in the killing?"

"No." Jill shook her head. "I'd be shocked to the core if Wayne remembered his own name, let alone Jim and myself. The kid went through so many foster homes...saw so many faces, so many names. Jim and I were just another set of invisible faces to the kid."

"Do you believe Richard Banks was killed by someone who intends to hurt you and Jim?" Bethany wanted to keep her questioning direct and straight. No veering off to the side.

"Yes, Bethany, I do. And that's why I'm sitting in this room." Jill's face became dead serious. "Bethany, Ben is a good man, but he doesn't have the experience Sarah has—or you. As long as I've lived in Hay Lake, there has never been a murder. Ben has never tried to solve a murder."

"What did Ben do before he became sheriff?" Bethany asked.

"Ben and his brother Jacob own a family-run hardware store. Ben's daddy was sheriff before him. Died of cancer. He was a good man...a real good man. Anyway, Ben ran for sheriff and was voted in. Been sheriff ever since. People like and respect him—"

"But he doesn't have any experience with murder."

Jill shook her head. "Bethany, Ben will get a bunch of dogs and go search the back woods. Good grief, whoever shot Richard Banks will not be back in the woods."

"I agree." Bethany had to admit that having a bunch of bored bloodhounds sniffing around autumn-soaked woods didn't seem practical. But Ben Nayes was sheriff, not Bethany. "Ben is concerned about Rhonda Banks."

"Well, that's a given." Jill folded her arms. She locked her eyes on the bay window for a few seconds and looked back at Bethany. "This stinks, Bethany...like a dead rat stuck between the teeth of a cat."

"A penny for your thoughts?" Bethany gently pressed. She needed to keep Jill on track.

"What do I have to lose? I've had enough tomatoes thrown at me to make an ocean of soup. Some of my jokes are so lame, my bag of laughs refuses to carry them."

Bethany smiled some. On any other occasion, it would have been enjoyable—even fun—to simply sit and talk with Jill. Jill was a tough schoolteacher, a brazen comedian who demanded clean humor, a loving wife, a committed businesswoman, and a loyal friend and neighbor. *Too bad we have to talk about murder. Jill Cunningham seems like the type of woman who could become a good friend.* "Jill, do you think Rhonda Banks killed her husband?"

"I'm considering it." Jill studied a pair of intelligent eyes clearly prepared for war. "Sarah was right. You are a smart woman."

"No. I'm simply putting myself in your shoes," Bethany informed Jill. "I'm also making assumptions based on what I saw and heard with my own eyes. Richard Banks showed up in a dangerously threatening mood. A man like that isn't married to a timid woman...at least, I wouldn't assume. If Rhonda Banks is a county commissioner, that tells me the woman is—"

"A bully," Jill finished for Bethany.

"Well, I would say a bold goal-setter...but underneath the business suits, yes, there is always the human nature aspect hiding." Bethany quickly scratched the tip of her nose, which always seemed to itch when her mind was chasing a bunch of loose thoughts. "Jill, why is Rhonda Banks a bully?"

"Richard and Rhonda Banks wanted to buy this land and build a mall on it," Jill explained without the slightest hesitation. "At the time, a petition stopped them. Richard and Rhonda Banks tried to delay the auction of the land, but their request was denied no matter how hard they tried and how many people they bribed...and trust me, Richard and Rhonda Banks greased a lot of palms and might have gotten away with sabotaging the land auction if Rhonda had been a county commissioner then. Long story short, the auction was held, and Jim and I bought the house and land you see before your very eyes."

"If Rhonda and Richard Banks were planning to build a mall, a property management company must have been involved, I'm assuming." Jill wasn't very familiar with how malls were built.

"Probably. Jim and I never stuck our noses down the rabbit hole that far," Jill confessed. "Jim and I put a target on our backs. Ever since we bought the land, Rhonda and Richard Banks have been hounding us. When Rhonda won a seat on the county commissioner seat...let's just say she devoted herself to making our lives very difficult." Jill let out a miserable sigh. "Humor helps keep me sane around here."

Bethany spoke but stopped when the cell phone inside of her purse rang. "Excuse me." She stood up and hurried to the bed, picked up her purse, and retrieved a fussy cell phone. She checked the incoming number but didn't recognize it. "Hello?" she asked.

"Leave Hay Lake or die. This is your only warning!" a threatening voice ordered. "Leave before it gets dark or die! Take your friend with you!"

Bethany heard the menacing voice quickly fade away as the call came to a sudden end. An icy chill ran through her heart. She turned away from Jill, walked over to the bay window, and looked out at the duck pond. *The snowman that chased Sarah is now chasing me. I can run or fight. If I stay and fight, I might die. I have until tonight to make my decision. There's no snow outside, but the snowman is out there, waiting in the darkness…*

chapter five

"The call came from a phone at a deserted gas station south of town," Ben told Bethany as he sat down at a round wooden kitchen table covered with an autumn leaf tablecloth. "There's a payphone that sits next to the store that still works. The gas station has been closed for years. It's a mystery why that old payphone still works."

Julie and Bethany were sitting at the table with Jill. Jim was leaning against a rustic kitchen counter lined with green and red plates holding homemade biscuits, muffins, donuts, and cookies. When Jill Cunningham loved to bake, Jim Cunningham adored his wife's habit. "Are you talking about the gas station that sits on the old trucking road?" Jim asked.

Ben nodded. "That's the one. No one goes up and down that road except truckers. That's the only road the truckers are allowed to use. County rules...a rule that actually makes sense for once." Julie's presence made Ben feel like he was back in high school, sitting close to the prettiest girl in his class. Bethany was beautiful, there was no question about that. But Julie, at least in Ben's eyes...wowzer! Julie was something amazing! But having a silly boyhood crush wasn't appropriate right now. A man was dead. Still, Ben couldn't help feeling like he was walking on cloud nine every time he looked into Julie's eyes.

"Someone would have had to have known that payphone was working," Bethany pointed out. It didn't take Bethany long to clearly see Ben was taken with Julie—any green-eared detective could see the man was smitten. She worried Ben might not be thinking as clearly as he needed to. "Right, Ben?"

"Huh? Oh, yeah, definitely." Ben quickly nodded. "I sent one of my guys out to have a look around. I don't think we'll find much."

"Like the dogs," Bethany added, and immediately regretted her snide remark. A pack of bored hound dogs had searched the thick, lush woods standing at the back of Jim's and Jill's property. The result? A bunch of tired noses. "I mean, I agree, Ben. Whoever used the payphone most likely left no clues." She quickly cleared herself from guilt.

Julie jumped into a deep hole to help her friend. "The question I'm wondering is why someone would call and threaten Bethany?" she asked to everyone instead of directing her question at Ben.

Jim rubbed a chubby chin. "That is a good question."

"I think I have the answer. Jim, bring Ben a cup of coffee really quick while I chew the fat."

"Sure, hon." Jim jumped to his chore. He found an old Charlie Brown coffee cup, filled the cup with hot coffee, and walked over to Ben. "Hot, now."

"Thanks, Jim. I could use a good cup of coffee." Ben accepted the coffee with a grateful hand. "Jill, the floor is yours."

Jill raised her right hand and pointed at Bethany and Julie. "My two friends are attached to Sarah Garland—"

"Sarah Spencer, hon," Jim corrected Jill, retaking his place beside the kitchen counter. He eyed a plate of homemade chocolate muffins and decided it was time to tickle his belly. A chocolate muffin fit all occasions...even murder.

"Just one!" Jill snapped. Jim jumped, blushed, and hurried to grab a muffin. "Okay," Jill continued. "Here is what I think. Bethany and Julie know Sarah. Whoever killed Richard Banks has to know who Sarah Garland—I mean, Spencer—is. Why else would that person call Bethany? And before anyone asks how Bethany's cell phone leaked into the wrong hands...well, Bethany called me from Alaska. All a person would have to do if they had access is check my phone records, right?"

"Could be." Ben nodded. "A person needs a warrant to have private phone records turned over to him."

"Phone records could have been hacked, or maybe an inside person works at the phone company that manages your records, Jill? There could be many possibilities. But I agree with you about Sarah. She has a famous reputation," Bethany pointed out. "Julie and I could be unexpected thorns." *Whoever killed Richard Banks did so right in front of Ben, which hints that maybe the shooter isn't worried about the local police. That leaves me and Julie. Maybe the shooter...the killer...somehow discovered that we're friends with Sarah and decided it's best if Julie and I should take a hike?*

Julie watched Ben take a sip of hot coffee. Ben was a handsome man—"dashing" was the word that came to Julie's mind. However, entertaining romance during murder was not appropriate. Besides, Julie was divorced. Why in the world would a man like Ben be interested in a woman who was divorced? Sure, Ben was divorced, but he divorced an ugly, bitter woman. What would Ben think if he discovered that Julie's husband had painted her as a black widow spider? "Maybe we should call Sarah?"

"I already did," Bethany confessed. "Sarah..." *Sarah what?* Bethany wondered. *Sarah basically told me to solve the murder and to call her if I needed any help. I objected, but Sarah insisted I take control. For whatever reason, Sarah seems to believe I'm a capable woman. She has a strange faith in me I can't see. I think maybe Sarah is also trying to teach me to stop comparing myself to her and seeing her as some kind of invincible woman. Sarah is flesh and blood, the same as me. Full of flaws, same as me. Vulnerable, same as me.*

"Sarah what, love?" Julie asked.

"Sarah told me to solve the murder," Bethany confessed, tossing a careful eye toward Ben. "No offense, Ben. I don't intend to step on your toes. With your permission, I would like to begin a private investigation. The man who called me sounded southern. That's a start, I guess."

"Now we're talking!" Jill shot to her legs and clapped her hands. "Now we're getting down to business! Right, Jim?"

"Right...business," Jim mumbled through a mouthful of chocolate muffin.

Ben took another sip of coffee and considered Bethany's suggestion for a minute. "Bethany, there are laws, but during my time as sheriff I've learned that most laws I'm forced to uphold are as crooked as a question mark. If you want to conduct your own investigation, I'll turn a blind eye and even offer you my help...out of view from the public eye." He glanced toward Julie. Law or no law, he wanted to be on the same team as the beautiful woman who was capturing his heart. Besides, he was sheriff, and the sheriff decided that was right. There was no crime in assisting a private investigator if the situation called for it. Every crooked politician in the state broke the law on a daily basis while portraying themselves as saints. Ben doubted that he and Julie would become Bonnie and Clyde if he assisted Bethany in her own private investigation.

"Now we're talking! You're a good man, Ben. Jim, get Ben a donut!" Jill exclaimed.

"No donut. Coffee is good." Ben grinned. Jill sure could get excited.

Bethany wanted to feel Jill's excitement, but she couldn't. A man was dead. Murder was ugly business. *Sarah's snowman is now haunting me. The snowman tried to run me away from Snow Falls when I arrived. The snowman followed me to ice mountain, to North Carolina, and now to Vermont. Yes, this murder isn't personal, but the snowman is involved, and Sarah knows it. Sarah defeated the snowman once, and now the snowman is back for revenge. Will I survive? I don't know.* "Ben, I appreciate your help. I think we're all going to step in and help each other."

"What's on your mind? Spill the beans, sister," Jill demanded, plopping back down on her seat. "We talked a little upstairs. Are you thinking Rhonda Banks is involved?" She nodded at Bethany. "Ben, Sarah told me this woman has sharp brains in her head. We'd be real smart to listen to her because Sarah has sharp brains herself."

"Sure does," Jim agreed, running a slow arm over his mouth. "Sarah is smart. But Jill, we're not stupid. We tell lame jokes sometimes, but the older we get...well, our bags of laughs collect lots of dust."

"I'm not implying we're stupid, Jim. But we have no experience with murder. Bethany has solved three murder cases this year."

"Julie, too," Bethany quickly added. "Julie and I have been a team since day one. Julie is just as smart, if not smarter than me."

Julie blushed a little. "Love, sometimes I feel like a puppy being dragged through the mud."

"Look, girls," Jill cut in. "What's important is that you're here and you have experience. No offense to my husband and Ben, but none of us have ever dealt with murder before. Ben has no experience. Jim and me, we're as green as grass when it comes to murder. Why, a cow could kill a bull with a tank, and we would think a pig was the guilty party."

"Well, Ben is sheriff—" Jim began.

"True, but Jill is right, Jim," Ben cut in. "I've never dealt with murder before. Richard Banks was shot right in front of me. Been wondering if that's a clear and direct message." He spoke in a voice that suddenly became tired. "Kill a man in front of the sheriff...that's a clear message that the killer thinks I'm a joke."

I guess Ben has been thinking along the same line as me. Maybe the man isn't as far out in right field as I believed. "We're going to have to work as a team," Bethany said. "I believe it's possible —and please know what I'm about to say is only a possibility —that the killer isn't working alone. If Rhonda Banks killed her husband, from what I learned of the woman so far, she isn't the type to operate alone. If Rhonda Banks isn't involved, we'll have to investigate a different path." *I sound like a lame duck. Good grief. If a private detective could grow feathers and quack, I'd be that person.*

"Love?" Julie asked, reading a troubled expression scarring Bethany's face. "What's wrong?"

"Oh...I'm just sitting here criticizing myself is all," Bethany moaned and slowly stood up, feeling like a tired old maid. "Sarah has faith I can handle this murder, and I'm trying to act like some lame duck detective. The truth is, I don't know what to do. Even if Rhonda Banks is involved, how can we prove it? If the woman is innocent, we have nothing to work with except a threatening phone call made from an old phone booth." Bethany shook her head. "Anyone could be the killer...maybe the killer is Wayne Tyler."

"I don't—" Jill objected.

"Or maybe the killer is some deranged hunter or an angry housewife or a frustrated farmer? Who knows?" Bethany finished in a tone that eased Jill's objection. Bethany nodded at Ben. "Everyone who knew Richard Banks needs to be questioned—family, friends, co-workers, and so on. Every skeleton in Richard Banks's closet needs to be dragged out into the open. The man's financial records need to be scrutinized. Rhonda Banks needs to be investigated. We're talking about a great deal of work and a great deal of manpower. And then there's a chance we could hit a dead end and come up empty-handed."

"Not to mention that if you and I are still here when the sun sets, love, we could become marked targets," Julie pointed out.

"Which means someone could be watching the bed and breakfast," Bethany added.

"What are you getting at, Bethany?" Jill demanded. "Are we supposed to throw up our hands and give up?"

"No, of course not." Bethany forced her mind to remain calm and focused. "All I'm implying is that we will not figure out who the killer is overnight, and our journey forward may be long, tedious, and very dangerous. But the one thing I am sure of is that Richard Banks was killed on your property for a reason."

"Rhonda Banks wants this land," Jill insisted.

"She sure does...more than Richard wanted this land," Jim confirmed.

Bethany nodded. "Rhonda Banks is our first rat to investigate. If we come up empty-handed, then we move on. Where? Who knows?" Bethany focused on Ben. "Ben, you're going to have to use all your resources to investigate Richard Banks."

"Consider it done," Ben promised.

"Julie." Bethany moved her eyes to her friend's worried face. "From this moment forward, you're at Ben's side."

"Love?" Julie asked, confused.

"You and Ben need to work as a team. I'm going to work with Jill and Jim. We'll get more done working in sets of teams." *That statement is only half true. The truth is, Julie will be safer with Ben...and maybe, who knows? Romance will bloom? Julie deserves to be loved by a good man, and Ben is obviously a good man. The way he looks at Julie...if only a man would look at me that way.* "Ben, you're going to have to camp here at the bed and breakfast."

"You can have the pumpkin room," Jill told Ben without the slightest hesitation. "And no hanky panky."

Both Ben and Julie blushed simultaneously. "Jill, you got it."

"Of course," Julie quickly added.

"Good. See to it you two stay that way." Jill turned to Bethany. "Okay, so we're a team. Good. What's our first order of business?"

"Ben will have to talk to Rhonda Banks," Bethany explained. "Hay Lake is a small community—about the size of Snow Falls, really. Ben told me Hay Lake doesn't have a detective."

"Dove Falls always sends a helping hand when needed," Ben cut in. "We've been trying to hire a detective, but no interested applicants have stepped up. It's not like we haven't been trying."

"Let's not ask for any outside help," Bethany told Ben. "If Rhonda Banks demands you ask for help, maybe that will prove she's innocent. If she agrees to keep the case local, that may show she is involved with the killing."

"Good thinking." Jill patted Bethany on her shoulder. "You're a thinking machine, Bethany, like me. I like that." She turned to Jim. "Jim, you best get our guns ready. I don't want to be walking around unarmed." She turned to Ben. "Jim and me both have a Glock 19 apiece. We took all the required training and have our licenses."

Jim grabbed another chocolate muffin. "I'll go upstairs and load up," he told Jill, hurrying out of the kitchen like a good husband.

Bethany looked at Julie. "Okay, honey, here we go again. Ready?"

"I was ready for hayrides and pumpkin patches and catching falling leaves..." Julie glanced toward the back door. Danger was coming out in the autumn afternoon in a deadly shadow. So much for a fun and relaxing vacation.

chapter six

Bethany watched Ben and Julie ride away in an old, rundown junker of a car. "Stay safe," she whispered to herself. Once Ben's old car was out of sight, she trained her eyes on a lush, autumn field that should have accompanied sweet dreams of pumpkin pies and fun corn mazes. Instead, the beautiful land standing before Bethany dripped with ominous whispers of danger and doom. "So beautiful...but murder taints beauty."

"It sure does." Jill nodded as she walked her eyes around. "Come on, let's take a walk around the property. Jim?"

"I'm right behind you." Jim stepped forward. "I'm locked and loaded, but to be honest, Jill, the shooter is not anywhere around. We've been living on this land a while now. I've trained my eyes to be aware of every inch of our land. I've trained my gut to know when something is out of place." He looked around as if he were a combat soldier trapped in enemy territory. "All morning I kept having a bad feeling...should have said something, but figured it was because of the meeting that took place last night. I didn't know Ben stepped up to bat for us. Anyway...Richard Banks is dead. I won't be losing any sleep over the guy's death, but the point is, he's dead. I guess that's the bad feeling that haunted me all morning. Now...my gut is at ease."

"Why didn't you tell me?" Jill fussed at her husband.

"Oh, just didn't want to worry you, I guess. Jill, you and I both kinda figured Rhonda Banks would make sure our request to turn our bed and breakfast into a Murder Mystery bed and breakfast would end up in the mud. I didn't want to add more dirt to the pig."

Jill reached out a loving hand and patted her husband's arm. "You old coot...I love you, too."

Bethany stared at Jim and Jill with curious eyes. *Jim and Jill are both a little eccentric, but they're also as normal as anyone I've ever met. They share a unique love rare in today's world—a love I find myself envious of. Jim loves Jill so deeply, and Jill loves Jim deeply. They're husband and wife, but they're also the best of friends.* "You two are very blessed to have each other," Bethany said before she could catch her mouth.

Jill patted Jim's arm again. "I'm blessed," she admitted, smiling into her husband's eyes. "I've been blessed from day one, Bethany. Jim has always been the kind of husband I dreamed of."

"Old and chubby," Jim joked. He leaned forward and kissed Jill on her cheek. "You're my dream come true, too, honey. Who else can bake pumpkin bread the way you do?"

Jill quickly poked Jim's chubby belly. "Maybe I shouldn't be such a wonderful cook." She grinned and quickly patted Jim's right hip. "Locked and loaded, right?" Jim nodded. "I've got my gun in my ankle holster. Bethany, how are you loaded?"

"Well, I own a Glock 17, but I was forced to leave my gun in Snow Falls."

"I assumed as much. Jim?"

Jim nodded, reached his right hand around his back, and pulled out a spare Glock 19 out from under his shirt. "Here you go, Bethany. You got a full clip. Take off the safety and fire. I don't think you need to be told how to handle this gun."

"I know how to handle a firearm," Bethany assured Jim, gratefully accepting the gun. To prove herself gun worthy, Bethany quickly carried out a safety check with skilled hands that even surprised her.

"Gal knows her stuff. Good. Let's check the property." Jill spoke in a way that exuded confidence in her husband and new friend. She retrieved her own gun and left the front porch. Jim pulled out his gun and followed his wife. Bethany tagged along after Jim, her eyes scanning her surroundings cautiously. "We'll check the back of the land first," Jill called out.

"Sounds good." Jim scanned his land with trained eyes. "It's going to rain tonight, Jill. Land will be wet tomorrow. You know how soggy the ground becomes. It'll be hard for anyone to sneak up on us without leaving obvious tracks."

"Good," Jill answered, heading around the side of her home—the side of her home that held a large wood pile. "Well, this is where the shooter seems to have been hiding." She stopped walking and looked around. "Jim, replay the scene for us."

"Well, had I been a hiding shooter..." Jim studied a tall wood pile that nearly reached up to the second floor of the house. The wood pile extended out about five feet. "In order to have had a clear shot at Richard, I would have had to be standing right here." He moved to the front corner of the wood pile. "I would have taken my shot...and then..." He turned around and studied the scenery. Nothing but an autumn-colored field and open woods stood behind the house. "It's a stretch to the wood line—a good two-minute run at full sprint. Whoever the shooter was had to be in awful good shape. Carrying a rifle while running isn't as easy as it looks."

Bethany surveyed the back of the house. *Jim's right. It is a good run to the woods. The shooter would have had to have taken a quick, deadly shot and run off quickly. But the question is...*

She walked back to the front of the wood pile and aimed her eyes toward the front driveway.

"What is it?" Jill asked. "You get a whiff of something?"

"I was wondering...if I was the shooter—the killer—I would have worried about being seen. Julie and Ron were inside the house. Did the shooter know their location?" *Julie and Ron could have been anywhere inside the house. The killer would have escaped into the woods, and Julie or Ron could have seen. I wonder if we're dealing with two killers or a killer who carried out a dangerous escape?*

"I wonder if the killer was a hired shooter, too...or not?" *So many questions. I guess this is why Sarah spent years learning how to become a homicide detective. It's not something a person becomes overnight, which makes me feel very inept. Yet, Sarah seems to believe I'm par for the job.*

"Now that's a question that hasn't entered the old noggin yet." Jill looked up toward a second-floor window. "There's the back hallway window. All the bedrooms and the one hallway bathroom cover the back of the house. The kitchen, reading room, and Jim's den cover the back of the downstairs. Don't see why Ron or Julie would have been in those rooms. Maybe the kitchen?"

Bethany focused back on the wood pile. "Okay, so let's pretend we're a shooter."

"Alright." Jill and Jim both nodded. Jim was wonderful—full of tender humility that warmed Bethany's heart. He wasn't the type of man who told a woman to stand down while he took charge. If a person—man or woman—had something important to say, he would listen with careful attention.

"Jim, Jill told me earlier that you were in the Marines."

"Long time back, but the training and instinct are still intact," Jim confirmed.

"If you were a shooter...well, walk me through what you believe might have happened." Bethany moved away from the wood pile to give Jim room.

Jim rubbed his chin with his left hand while securing a powerful gun with his right hand. "Well, the way I see it is, the shooter would have sneaked up to the house from the woods. But remember, and this is something I didn't tell Ben because, well, Ben is a close friend and a good cop, but he's not trained in homicide. Anyway, keep in mind me and Jill were in and out of the house all morning. We didn't see anyone. Richard Banks was the intended target of the shooting, and that tells me that the shooter knew two things."

"Tell her, Jim," Jill ordered proudly. "My husband has brains in his head."

Jim blushed some. Jill always bragged on him. "Thanks, honey...anyway, here's what I think. The shooter was after Richard Banks, which tells me he knew Richard was on his way to our property. But if that's so, how did the shooter get here so fast? No—the shooter must have been waiting. We live a good piece out, Bethany, as you saw yourself when Ron rode you in. So, number one: the shooter had to have known Richard was coming to the property. Number two: the shooter wasn't worried about Ben. Why? Oh, maybe for many reasons...or maybe because the shooter knew he had a clear escape route."

"The shooter knew Richard Banks was coming to our land and knew how to escape," Jill summarized Jim's words.

Jim nodded toward the front yard. "The shooter takes a clear aim at Richard Banks, kills his target, and makes a mad dash back to the woods," he continued. "Now, Ben had those old hound dogs sniff around. To some people, Ben's actions seemed green-eared and a waste of time, but I paid attention. Those hound dogs should have caught scent of something but didn't. Bethany, I can stand right here and leave my scent, and I assure you, a trained set of hound dogs would track down my scent. Ben wasn't so dumb in having those dogs brought out to the land."

Bethany soaked in every word Jim spoke. *I know little about hound dogs. At first, I thought Ben's actions were foolish, but Jim seems to think otherwise. I would be smart to pay attention. Sarah may think I'm smart—and maybe I have survived three murder cases—but I'm still a green-eared rookie, and the snowman that haunted Sarah is out there somewhere in the autumn winds. I can feel him. Sarah's snowman has become my monster.*

"What does that mean? The shooter somehow destroyed his scent?"

"Can't never get rid of your scent, Bethany," Jim explained. "Oh, I suppose in today's world there might be ways, but when I was in the jungle, sweat, toothpaste, underarm deodorant...simple things like that could mark a man for death. You would be amazed at how far the wind can carry a simple scent." He took a brown boot and kicked the bottom of the wood pile. "A man can sit down in the jungle and leave a few droplets of sweat on the ground. The scent of his sweat can linger, lead the enemy right to him. Men train their noses to become, well, the noses you'd find on a hound dog."

"Jim, cut to the cheese," Jill pleaded. "What are you getting at?"

"The shooter didn't lean against the wood pile to take his shot," Jim confirmed. "I saw the hound dogs sniff the wood pile...nothing. Also, there weren't any tracks on the ground, and as you can see, Bethany, this part of the ground is bare, mostly dirt, because we stack tons of wood right here. But"—Jim nodded at the ground—"if you look closely at the ground, you'll see that it almost looks swept. Didn't mention this to Ben because what good would it have done? Maybe I should have opened my mouth more? I meant no disrespect."

"I can see that," Bethany promised Jim, and turned her eyes down toward a patch of ground that was indeed mostly dirt. At first, the ground simply appeared normal. Nothing unusual appeared in the bright, glowing light. But the more Bethany stared at the ground, the more she seemed to notice how smooth certain parts of the dirt appeared compared to other areas. She used her eyes to draw a straight line...and yes, the line her eyes drew appeared smooth while the dirt around the line was rugged and disturbed. "Jim, what are you—"

"A professional," Jim confessed, allowing a deep worry he had been hiding to finally enter the light of day. "Richard Banks took a clear shot to the heart. Instant death. The hound dogs came up blank...the ground around the wood pile...certain parts of the ground at least." He nodded at the ground and made a line with his left pointer finger that matched the line Bethany's eyes had created. "It looks swept. Whoever killed Richard Banks came in, did the job, and got out. In the jungle, as a Marine, I was trained to strike fast and fade out fast."

Bethany grew silent for a moment as her mind explored Jim's words. *A professional killer was hired to kill Richard Banks. The killer knew Richard Banks would visit Jim's and Jill's property. Did the killer know Ben was going to be on sight? Maybe, maybe not? The killer wasn't concerned about Ben. The killer shot Richard Banks and escaped. And now, here I stand.* "So this leads us back to Rhonda Banks," she pointed out.

Jim nodded. "Maybe Ben isn't trained for homicide, Bethany, but he's got a good head on his shoulders. Ben is a people person. He can read someone like a book within seconds of meeting that person. When you suggested Ben question Rhonda Banks, I knew you made a smart move."

"I agree with Jim. Ben is good at reading people," Jill agreed. She bent down and tossed her gun into an ankle holster. "I don't think we need our guns, Jim. I'm getting the feeling that we're all alone out here except for the cows." She drew in a deep breath. "Come on, let's go back inside and talk. I'll make us some coffee. We're not going to find anything out here."

Jim walked his eyes around a beautiful landscape. "Jill, Richard Banks was killed on our property. If Rhonda Banks has her way, we might be blamed for the killing. That woman is meaner than a hungry cobra. I didn't think she would take matters this far, assuming she's involved. If she is—"

"I know, honey, I know." Jill took Jim's hand. "Bethany, I guess you didn't expect to walk into another murder case. I'm sure glad you're here."

Bethany wasn't so sure she could share Jill's confidence. She was having a bad feeling that Richard Banks wasn't the only intended target. *It'll be dark soon. When the sun sets, the snowman will come out of hiding...and attack.*

chapter seven

"Hospital?"

Ben nodded as he took a sip of hot coffee. "As soon as Rhonda Banks identified her husband's body, she collapsed. Dr. Rovinger informed me that shock was the culprit." He shook his head. "Rhonda Banks has been transferred to Dove Falls. I talked to a Dr. Smith in Dove Falls who told me Rhonda Banks's condition is stable. That's all the information I was given. I'll drive down to Dove Falls tomorrow and see what's going on."

"'Shock' my foot in a hind box," Jill huffed. She dipped a wooden soup spoon down into a deep brown cooking pot full of delicious Brunswick stew, then quickly wiped her hands on a yellowish-brown apron that had been handmade in the year 1964. "Seems to me like Rhonda Banks wanted to get out of being questioned."

"Could be," Ben agreed. "Uh...how did things go with Bethany?" Bethany and Julie were upstairs washing up for dinner.

"Bethany is one smart cookie," Jill affirmed. "I think we made a lot of progress today." She nodded at her husband, who was perched at the kitchen table sipping on a hot cup of coffee. "Jim is a smart cookie, too."

"I know he is," Ben agreed. "I think Jim knows more than he's telling me. Right, Jim?"

Jim stiffened a little. "Well, maybe I have been keeping a few thoughts to myself, Ben. No disrespect toward you. I'm just gnawing on some bones that taste like assumption more than facts is all."

"Well, we're all gnawing on assumption right now." Ben sighed. "Judge Weathers refused to give me a search warrant today. I can't look into Richard's personal files. As a matter of fact, Richard Banks's files have been placed under lock and key. I ran Richard through the National Crime Data Base, or the NCDB, as we call it."

"And?" Jill asked anxiously

"Nothing but the basics. Richard Banks doesn't have a criminal record, Jill. He had two traffic tickets that were issued to him in Boston years back before moving to Hay Lake. In college, the guy was arrested at a political protest for punching a security guard, but the charges were eventually dropped. That's it. Name...rank...social security number. Right, Jim?"

Jim sighed. "Yeah, that's the way of it."

"Did you find any personal contacts?" Jill pressed. "Anything?"

"Of course there are personal contacts, Jill, but as I said, Richard Banks's records have been locked up tighter than superglue sticking to a piece of paper. It's no secret that Judge Weathers was friends with Richard Banks. Who knows? Maybe the guy is connected to the killing?"

"Did you talk to anyone at the bank? Mr. Goshen?" Jim asked, keeping his voice easy.

"I talked to Mr. Goshen." Ben nodded. "He was more interested in drooling over Julie. Julie noticed the obvious. She really helped me get some information out of a tight-lipped mule."

"Oh?" Jill rushed over to the kitchen table. "What?"

"Well," Ben took another sip of coffee, "Mr. Goshen—"

"The bank president," Jim quickly added.

Ben nodded. "Mr. Goshen told me and Julie he was getting ready to fire Richard Banks. Richard was in charge of the loan department."

"The skunk." Jill scowled.

"Yeah, I agree." Ben put down his coffee. "Mr. Goshen confirmed that Richard Banks was allowing unqualified business loans to be given to businesses operating outside of Hay Lake. The bank in question is a small community bank. The loans Richard Banks was allowing were putting financial strain on the bank, and Mr. Goshen confessed he was certain Richard Banks was not only conducting illegal transactions but was attempting to ruin the bank."

Jim rubbed his chin. "What businesses are we talking about, Ben? Construction? Retail? Restaurant?"

"Land development," Ben confirmed. "Three separate companies are involved. Each company, according to Mr. Goshen—and we have Julie and her flirty eye to thank for the information—is in different areas." He reached into the front pocket of his sheriff's shirt and pulled out a piece of paper. "The MacMillin Land Development Company is in Montpelier, the Foster Land Development Company is in Newark, and the Siclough Land Development Company...hmm, wonder if I spelled that name right? No matter...the company is in Detroit."

Jim rubbed his chin again. "What do these companies build? Shopping centers, medical offices…"

"Shopping centers," a clear voice spoke. Jim turned in his seat and spotted Bethany and Julie in the kitchen doorway. "All three land development companies build shady shopping centers," Bethany continued. "The MacMillin Company has been shut down twice for code violations—"

"And from hiring illegal aliens instead of legal citizens,"

Julie added. "Some of the illegal aliens hired were connected to drug cartels in Mexico."

"That's right." Bethany nodded. "The Foster Company is under investigation for human trafficking and drugs. The Siclough Company is being investigated for having ties to what appears to be a mafia family in Detroit."

"Goodness." Jill shook her head. "I always knew Richard Banks was up to no good!"

"Mind me asking how you came across this information?" Ben asked Bethany.

"I spent the last hour upstairs on the phone with Peter. Peter is Sarah Spencer's close friend. He's a retired homicide detective running a private investigation firm in Los Angeles," Bethany explained.

"Peter is terrific," Julie told Ben. "You have to meet Peter to understand how terrific he is, like an old, lovable teddy bear."

"And smarter than I'll ever be," Bethany confessed.

"Well, thank goodness we have friends in high places!" Jill clapped her hands together. "Now we're making progress. Everyone, sit down. I'll serve dinner and we'll talk more." She nodded at the kitchen window. Cold pellets of rain were striking the window. "Night has arrived, and you girls are still here. Not sure who called you, Bethany, but your being here makes a loud and bold statement. Whoever called you isn't going to like that you and Julie stayed. We have lots to talk about."

Jim tossed a worried eye at Bethany and Julie. Were the two women now in danger? He feared the answer was yes. "Whoever killed Richard Banks could easily take a shot at any of us if we get too close. From here on out, I think we need to use extra caution."

"Well, we set up the wires around the house with the cans attached," Jill said. "I trapped every window with cans and bottles. The alarm system is set. The inside generator we spent so much money on is in working condition. I think we're okay for tonight, Jim." She walked back to an old-fashioned Westinghouse stove. "Don't worry about tomorrow. Tomorrow will take care of itself when it arrives. Tonight, we need to review what we know."

Jim knew his wife was right. "You always had a sensible head, honey." He smiled.

"And you're justified in worrying whether anyone might take a quick shot at us, too," Jill added. "That thought has crossed my mind once or twice...or a million times."

Bethany began to speak but stopped when the kitchen telephone rang.

"I'll get it." Jim stood up and hurried over to a brown phone hanging beside the refrigerator. "Hello?"

"I killed Richard Banks. Do as I say, or you're next," a threatening voice demanded. "Get rid of your new friends or your wife dies. I'm an excellent shot, Jim. I don't miss. You have until tomorrow at noon to get rid of your friends or you will end up a widower. And tell your cop friend to back off or he's dead."

Jim looked over at his wife—at the most beautiful face he had ever seen. A face that was his home. "You're not going to leave me and my wife alone...whoever you are."

Ben jumped to his feet and scrambled over to Jim before Bethany and Julie could move. Jill held up a quick hand that told the two women to remain where they were standing. "You have until tomorrow at noon or I'll pay you a visit, Jim."

"No deal." Jim shook his head. "Whoever you are, you intend to kill me and my wife. You just want me to get rid of everybody to make sure the body count is low. I don't back down from bullies, and neither does my wife. We'd rather die than run like cowards."

"That's right!" Jill hollered.

"I'm not kidding!" the voice hissed. "Don't push at me,

Jim. I strike hard. Richard Banks felt my wrath today. Don't make the same mistake."

"You'll have to kill me and my wife before we leave our land, you hear!" Jim's voice erupted with a righteous anger that shocked Bethany and Julie. The humble little jolly fella with the plump belly had a temper. "You want a fight? You got one! You hear me, punk! Do you—"

Before Jim could finish, the caller brought the conversation to a close. "He hung up." Jim slammed the phone receiver he was holding down with a hard hand.

Ben pulled out a black cell phone and made a call. "It's Ben. Someone called the Cunningham's home. Get on the horn with the phone company and discover where the call came from." Ben gave an alert deputy the time. "Wake up whoever you must. Is that clear? Good." Ben put his cell phone away. "Jim, did you by any chance recognize the caller?"

"Deep voice...sounded like a man in his mid to late forties. Had a real thick southern accent."

"Texas?" Ben asked.

"No. More like Georgia. Sounded like a close friend I served with in the Marines from a little town in North Georgia called Blue Ridge. Jill and I visited the town once. Real nice place." Jim walked over to his wife and put a loving arm around her. "Whoever I was speaking to told me to get rid of Bethany and Julie or he would kill Jill. I was told I have until noon tomorrow to obey."

"Do you know anyone from Georgia?" Ben asked Jim and Jill. Bethany and Julie listened closely.

"Just my friend from the Marines. But he died two years ago of cancer," Jim explained, his voice saddened.

"That's right. Wiley McClure died of cancer two years back in his home. Jim and I were present, and Wiley's family was also present. You can call them to find out. Wiley's wife, bless her soul, is a wonderful woman," Jill added. "Edna can testify that Jim and I were present at Wiley's death."

"We don't know anyone else from Georgia, Ben," Jim said with a sigh. "Wiley was a real good friend. I was sad to see him go."

Jill squeezed her husband's hand. "The older we get, honey." Jim nodded in agreement.

Bethany stared at Jim and Jill for a minute. *The person who called me had a southern accent, too.* "The man who called me—"

"Southern accent. I remember," Ben cut Bethany off. "I should have asked more questions about the call, Bethany. I guess I'm learning as I go."

"Don't be hard on yourself, Ben," Jim demanded. "You've never had to work on a homicide case before, and Dove Falls isn't offering any help." He looked at Bethany. "Looks like the same man who called you just called me, Bethany. We could have a match."

"I think we have a match. The question is, who is the caller, and how is the caller connected to Richard Banks?" Bethany rubbed the back of her neck with a tired hand. "Jill, mind if I have a cup of coffee?"

"I'll make you a cup. Sit down. Julie, you sit down, too. You and Bethany look worn down to the bone." Jill hurried to prepare two cups of hot coffee.

Bethany took a seat at the kitchen table, but Julie remained standing. "May I share a thought with everyone. Something I've been wondering about?" she asked nervously. "Before I do, please remember that I'm not a detective."

"Honey, you spill the beans. Whatever you got to say must be important," Jill demanded, handing Julie a cup of coffee. "Careful, it's hot."

"Thank you." Julie gingerly accepted her cup of coffee and looked around at four staring faces. "Well, I've been thinking about Rhonda Banks and wondering if she is not connected to the killing of Richard Banks." Julie's British accent thickened, which happened when she became nervous.

"Oh?" Jill hurried a cup of coffee over to Bethany and plopped down beside her. "The floor is yours, honey."

"It sure is." Jim hurried over to Jill and sat down. "What's making you think that Rhonda Banks may not be involved with the killing?"

Bethany stared at her friend. What thoughts were coursing through Julie's mind? *Julie is a brilliant woman. I'm not the only person involved in this case, and I'm blessed to have Julie at my side. Sometimes I forget Julie understands murder as well as I do.* "What are you thinking, honey?"

Julie cleared her throat. "Well, love, I've been thinking about how Richard Banks died."

"Shot to death," Jill confirmed.

Julie nodded and set her coffee down on a crowded kitchen counter lined with delicious baked goods. "Well, I know we all agree that the shooter had to have known Richard Banks would visit your property. We all assume that perhaps Rhonda Banks set her husband up for murder?"

"That's what we're leaning on," Ben confessed.

"Yes...however…" Julie took a second to secure her nervous thoughts. Bethany was the detective, not her. However, Julie knew that if Sarah had confidence in Bethany, Sarah's confidence reflected onto Julie. Julie and Bethany were a team. "The killing happened so fast, and the shooter escaped without being seen or caught. Also, the hound dogs you had brought to the property, Ben, came up empty-handed…well-empty-nosed. I've been wondering how a shooter could get onto the land so quickly? There's only the one driveway. What if the shooter has been around for a while?"

"A while?" Jill asked.

"Someone called and threatened Bethany and Jim. Whoever that person is seems very confident."

"Which means that the caller must know our land, is that it?" Jim cut in.

"Well, how else would the caller kill anyone?" Julie asked. "Ben and I left your property today, Jim, and now we're back. The caller—if he's the shooter—could have taken a shot at anyone today but instead—"

"The shooter is trying to scare people off," Jim finished for Julie and rubbed his chin. "Jill, honey, you better go make another pot of coffee. It's going to be a long night."

chapter eight

"I can't believe I'm doing this," Bethany whispered under her breath as she walked down a silent hallway lined with closed hospital doors. The hallway smelled of a strong disinfectant that made Bethany's stomach feel queasy. "I hate hospitals."

A middle-aged nurse named Penny Davis spotted a lovely woman with red hair approaching the nursing station where she was parked. The Dove Falls Memorial Hospital wasn't exactly a thriving metropolis hospital in downtown Boston or Hartford. It was more or less a dinky little brick building offering a few medical services that the medical station in Hay Lake didn't, or couldn't. Dove Falls was one step up from Hay Lake—a step that came in the form of a Chick-Fil-A and a miserable movie theater that showed junk movies. Penny hungered for the old days. Oh well. At least she still had her church.

"Can I help you?" she asked the woman warmly.

Bethany approached a pleasant-looking woman with deep brown hair that complimented an intelligent face, a face Bethany wasn't sure she would be able to deceive. "Uh..." *It's way past midnight, and here I am standing in a hospital. I must be insane.* "I'm not sure. I was told my cousin was here. I just drove up from Buffalo."

"Who is your cousin?" Penny asked.

"Rhonda Banks. I was told her husband was killed...awful," Bethany told Penny in a voice she hoped sounded sorrowful, shaking her head.

Penny simply smiled. "Nice try, ma'am," she told Bethany. "I can't tell you how many reporters I've turned away today. The last reporter was an uncle from Nashville."

"Oh..." *Nice going, Bethany. You just crash-landed before you even had air under your wings.* "That obvious, huh?"

"Afraid so." Penny held her smile. She didn't mind chasing off a reporter. The night shift could get boring. "Mrs. Banks has been marked as off limits. Sorry."

"Well..." Bethany glanced around. No other nurses were present. She turned her focus back to Penny. Penny seemed like a pleasant woman—a Christian woman. "Can you keep a secret?"

"Depends," Penny answered and motioned around. "Patient safety comes first."

Bethany nodded and removed her identification from a white purse. "My name is Bethany Lights. I live in Snow Falls, Alaska." Bethany handed Penny a fancy new driver's license and then, to her surprise, confessed her situation in clear detail. "My friends and I concluded that Mrs. Banks isn't involved in the killing, but her life could be in danger. I was hoping I could speak to her. If you need to call the local sheriff, that would be fine."

"Bethany"—Penny handed Bethany back her driver's license—"our local sheriff is about as helpful as a rat jumping from a sinking ship. We have a new detective in town, but she's about as nice as a scorpion." She studied Bethany's face and spotted a pair of honest eyes staring at her—eyes that needed a friend instead of an enemy. "Listen, I have to use the bathroom. I've already dispensed patient medications for tonight—a total of five patients. All that's left for me to do is a little charting and drinking lots of coffee to stay awake." She glanced around. The floor was silent. She was the only nurse on the clock. Betty and Mandy were pulling the ER shift. Dr. Ailes was probably in the staff lounge, arguing with his ex-wife over their teenage son. The x-ray and lab people—two people—were probably sitting around twiddling their thumbs. Yes, the night shift at Dove Falls Memorial Hospital was about as eventful as watching paint dry.

Penny couldn't remember the last time a true emergency arose. The only patients on her floor were four elderly old men admitted after falling in a lake and catching a terrible cold, and Rhonda Banks. "Rhonda Banks is in that room." She quickly pointed to a closed door. "When I enter the room and chase you out, don't be upset by my attitude—it's all an act. You have ten minutes, so make it count."

Bethany felt a wave of relief crash down on her heart. "I will, I promise...and thank you."

"I sense that you're an honest woman." Penny glanced around. "Ten minutes," she repeated, and then called the ER. "Betty, I'm on bathroom break for ten. I'm routing all calls to you until I get back. Okay, thanks." She quickly set down the phone and then rushed off to a small bathroom.

"Thank you," Bethany whispered, hurrying to a closed door. She drew in a deep breath, prayed for guidance, and entered a dimly lit hospital room that smelled of disinfectant and dusty silence. A grumpy-faced, gray-haired woman was sitting up on a lumpy bed holding a cell phone in her hand. When the woman spotted Bethany, she quickly tucked the cell phone under a white blanket.

"Mrs. Banks?"

"Who are you? My room is off limits!" Rhonda Banks barked.

Bethany quickly stepped into the room and approached the hospital bed. Boy, she thought, Rhonda Banks sure resembled a grumpy-faced spider. The woman's eyes dropped with venom and cruelty—but also with fear. Rhonda Banks was a scared woman. *Maybe I should just leave? This woman doesn't deserve my help...but maybe I can get some information out of her. I put my life in danger leaving Jim's and Jill's home.* "Mrs. Banks, you don't know me—"

"Get out. I'm not speaking to any report—"

"Mrs. Banks, I'm not a reporter," Bethany cut Rhonda off sternly. *No heart monitor. No intravenous line. The woman is wearing a pink robe, which means someone she trusts has been here.* She studied Rhonda with observant eyes. *This woman doesn't need to be in a hospital. She's hiding out.* "Mrs. Banks, I'm here because I believe your life is in danger, and now I can see you believe the same. At first, I thought you allowed yourself to be admitted to a hospital because you wanted to create a public image that would gain you sympathy. Now I can see that's not the case."

"Get out or—"

"You don't know who killed your husband, do you?" Bethany asked, keeping her voice stern. "Your husband had a lot of enemies, didn't he?"

"I said—"

"And you're scared. You're scared you might be the next person lying in a cold morgue, right?" Bethany asked.

Rhonda stared at Bethany with angry eyes that quickly diminished into shaky fear. "Whoever you are...yes, I'm scared. My husband was killed, and I may be next. Now...get out!"

"Mrs. Banks, did it occur to you that I might be a killer?" Bethany asked, deliberately paralyzing Rhonda with fear. "The press cannot enter your room. How do you know I didn't kill the duty nurse? How do you know I'm not here to kill you?" She reached into her purse with a quick hand.

"No! Please!" Rhonda cried out in horror.

"Relax." Bethany pulled out her cell phone. "Mrs. Banks,

I'm not a killer. I'm here because I believe your life is in danger." She called Ben. "Alright, Ben, make it quick because I have less than ten minutes."

"Rhonda?" Ben called out.

"Ben Nayes?" Rhonda's fearful expression turned into muddy confusion. "What is this—"

"Listen, Rhonda. I'm sitting outside the hospital," Ben explained. "The scene is clear. If you have any sense in your head, you will leave right now. I won't be able to guarantee your safety after tonight. Someone has called both the woman standing before you and Jim Cunningham and threatened them. We don't know that person. We doubt you do, either."

"Of course I don't, you idiot!" Rhonda snapped. "When I found out my husband had been killed, I nearly died myself. Richard has a lot of enemies, all right? There, I said it. But I'm not saying anything anyone with a brain doesn't already know."

"You're not innocent, Rhonda," Ben barked.

"Of course I'm not. Why do you think I'm so scared?" Rhonda barked back.

"Rhonda, you better leave Hay Lake and leave fast. But before you do, the woman standing before you has a few questions. Please answer her questions," Ben ordered. "And before you object, you better show some appreciation to her. My friend demanded she be allowed to help you because, as horrible as you are, Rhonda, my friend didn't want to see an innocent person die."

Rhonda lifted her eyes to study Bethany's face. "What do you want to know?" she snapped.

"Nothing personal, I assure you." Bethany checked the time. "Mrs. Banks, I'm sorry about your husband. Murder is an awful creature to become haunted by."

"Get to the point," Rhonda snapped again.

Bethany nodded. "The man who called and threatened me

and Mr. Cunningham had a deep southern accent. Do you know anybody who might have such an accent?"

Rhonda clearly tensed up. "My husband was dealing with a man...a shady man from Atlanta. I told him not to get involved with that awful man, but did he listen? No. Our goal was to take over Hay Lake—a pathetic little lake town—and we failed." Disgust temporarily replaced fear on her face. "A pathetic little lake town filled with nobody's—"

"Do you have a name for the man your husband was associated with?" Bethany asked, remaining sharp and focused. She didn't have time to dive into dramatics. *I risked my life leaving Jim and Jill's property. Ben did, too. We made it seem as if Ben was arresting me just in case anyone was watching. Maybe someone was watching...the killer, maybe? No one followed Ben's car to Dove Falls, that much is certain. This entire case is filled with question marks.*

Rhonda locked eyes with Bethany. "If you're smart, you'll leave Hay Lake and never look back. That's what I will do. I'm through wasting my time with Jim and Jill Cunningham. I told Richard building a mall on that awful land was a waste of time, but he insisted. The truth is, I didn't care about that land. Richard pestered me and pestered me...he kept sinking our money into worthless projects. I could have had Hay Lake under my thumb within a year's time if it hadn't been for...well, Richard is dead."

"And you don't care, do you?" Bethany let a quick emotion slip.

"No," Rhonda answered in a direct, honest voice. "Richard never loved me. At first, perhaps I loved Richard, but through the years, he caused the love I once felt for him to die. Can you understand that?"

"Actually, I can," Bethany told Rhonda in a tone that caused the woman to lean back. "Mrs. Banks, do you have a name?"

"No."

Bethany studied Rhonda's eyes. Was the woman offering an honest answer? *The answer to my question is yes.* "Mrs. Banks, I don't know you, but your reputation is one that people despise, and—"

"I don't care what people think of me!"

"I risked my life to tell you I believe your life is in danger, regardless of what kind of woman you are...and it's apparent your reputation is accurate in all forms. But I had to warn you." Bethany stood still. "I was hoping in return you might help me."

"Yes, yes, it's always you scratch my back and I'll scratch yours. You're no saint. Now get out! I need to get dressed!" Rhonda pointed at the door. "I've said enough. I'm through talking."

"Rhonda," Ben's voice came through the cell phone Bethany was holding. "I'm outside watching the front parking lot. I'll watch you until you leave. After that, I'm going back to Hay Lake. You can come back to Hay Lake and I can try to protect you, but I can't guarantee your safety."

"I'm leaving the United States," Rhonda snapped. "You'll never see me again. My brother is making all the arrangements, and—" Rhonda slid to a stop, realizing she was letting too much slip. "Get out!"

"Mrs. Banks, I feel very sorry for you," Bethany spoke in a low voice filled with sadness. "You're going to be running for the rest of your life. And why?"

She turned and left the room as Penny appeared. "She's all yours," Bethany said, putting her hand on the nurse's shoulder. "If you ever travel to Alaska, stop and see me. You'll always have a friend there."

Penny glanced at Rhonda, who was quickly uncovering herself. "Maybe someday I will get to Alaska." She smiled. "Bye."

"Bye." Bethany hurried out of the room and made her way down the quiet hallway. When she reached the front lobby—a medium-sized room designed to resemble a lousy art gallery filled with uncomfortable furnishings and ugly artwork—she saw a shadowy man sitting in a stiff chair perched beside an empty wooden desk that usually housed a nice old woman who answered calls.

"Hello, Bethany," a voice spoke in a tone that caused a creepy chill to run down Bethany's back.

Bethany quickly threw her eyes toward a pair of glass sliding doors. Ben was parked outside in the front parking lot. Could he see her? No.

"Who are you?" Bethany asked. The man sitting in the shadows didn't speak with a southern drawl.

"You're in way over your head, Bethany. Back off and go back to Snow Falls. I'll handle this case," the man spoke and slowly stood up. "The shooter is not important, Bethany...and not who you think. But if you persist in sticking your nose where it doesn't belong, you might cause a great deal of trouble for yourself."

Bethany squinted. The man speaking to her was wearing a gray hat and a gray trench coat. She couldn't see his face. "My friends are in trouble. I won't leave them."

"I admire you for that, but rest assured, Jim and Jill Cunningham are in no danger." The man raised his eyes. "*Yet*. You need to leave, Bethany. You have until tomorrow night. I'll guarantee your safety until then. After that, no more warnings. Take Julie Walsh and leave. If you see me again...I may not be so nice, understand?" With those words, the shadowy man walked toward Bethany, paused, and vanished down the hallway.

Bethany watched the man slowly disappear down the hall and rushed outside into a hard rain, finding Ben. She jumped into Ben's old car and informed him of her encounter. Ben grabbed his gun and burst into the hospital...but came up empty-handed. The shadowy man had simply vanished, leaving Bethany with a choice: leave or die.

chapter nine

Bethany rubbed a pair of exhausted eyes as a blast of chilly morning wind smelling of thick chimney smoke struck her face. Bright autumn leaves were being tossed about in the wind like crying children instead of laughing hearts. A low, gray damp from the rain stood overhead, drowning out any hope of sunshine. Cold milk cows stood off in the distance looking bored—or miserable, Bethany couldn't decide which. *Boy, I'm in a depressed mood. Sure, the sky is gray, but the land is still beautiful, and eventually the sun will come out. Yes, I can almost smell the winter snow, but the lush voice of autumn is still thick in the air. I suppose I'm depressed because I'm confused. I have no idea what's going on. Last night was foolish. I should have never risked going to see Rhonda Banks. Me and my stupid ideas.*

"Morning, love." Julie stepped out onto the front porch, hugging a hot cup of coffee.

"How did you sleep?" Bethany asked, turning to face her lovely friend, who was wearing a heavy brown sweater.

"Not good, I'm afraid," Julie confessed, quickly scanning the land. "The land is beautiful...peaceful. Reminds me of a little village in the English countryside I used to visit as a little girl. At times..." Julie paused, took a sip of coffee, and sighed.

"At times what, honey?" Bethany asked. The chilly morning winds were doing a lousy job of waking her up, but the winds felt refreshing—like a splash of cold water striking a tired face. She wrapped her arms around a heavy green sweater and waited for Julie to finish.

"Oh, at times I miss England," Julie confessed. "I miss the countryside, the coast...and I miss London."

"Honey, I get it. I'm sorry." Bethany lowered her head.

Julie eyed Jim and Jill's land. "The snowman Sarah wrote about, it's following us now. I can feel it, love...deep in my heart. Some people might call me insane. So be it."

"I feel the snowman, too. It took me a while to put my finger on it." Bethany stood silent for a minute before continuing. "The murders in Snow Falls, on Ice Mountain, in North Carolina...the murders are all attached to the snowman."

"But why us?" Julie begged. "Or better yet, love, why you?"

"Sarah and Amanda defeated the snowman once...now the snowman wants revenge." Bethany felt a cold chill run down her back. "The snowman attacked silently at first, but now we're aware of it." Bethany turned back to Julie. "I thought I felt the snowman on Ice Mountain, but I couldn't be sure. Our fight in North Carolina happened so quickly that we barely had time to breathe...and honestly, honey, it seemed like we were more or less watchers than participants in North Carolina. The nightmare in North Carolina felt like—"

"The snowman was just warming up?" Julie shivered as she asked the question.

Bethany reluctantly nodded. "The snowman is everywhere...we're not safe," she concluded. "I remember Sarah telling me the story about how she accompanied

Amanda to a remote lodge north of Snow Falls. An evil woman was waiting there."

"That woman released a virus into the air that nearly killed Sarah and Amanda."

"Yes," Bethany confirmed miserably. "Sarah and Amanda had to soak their bodies in a scalding hot spring. They were nearly killed by a grizzly bear...so much happened to them. You wouldn't be able to tell it by looking at our friends, though, would you?"

"No." Julie shook her head. "Sarah and Amanda possess a true talent. They can hide what they are feeling so deep that not even I can see it, and I'm talented at reading people's emotions, love."

Bethany spoke but stopped when Ben stepped through the front door, bringing a cup of coffee and a donut with him. "Morning." He yawned.

"Morning." Julie offered a polite smile. "Did you rest well?"

"No," Ben confessed. "I couldn't stop kicking myself for losing a deadly suspect."

"Ben, it wasn't your fault," Bethany said firmly. "The man waiting for me, he wasn't your average man."

"Be that as it may, I'm still a law man and I have a duty...and last night, I failed." Ben took a quick sip of coffee. "I want you two on the first flight out—"

"No deal," Bethany and Julie cut Ben off at the same time. Bethany quickly took over. "Julie and I have discussed the situation. We're not leaving, Ben. Whoever the man I met last night was, he knew who I was and who Julie was. I don't enjoy being scared off, and I have a bad feeling that even if Julie and I leave, the man waiting for me at the hospital last night will show up in Alaska. It's better for everyone if we remain together as a team."

"I agree, and I trust in Bethany's gut feeling," Julie chimed in. "Ben, I trust Bethany with my life. Bethany and I have become closer than sisters in a short time. That may be hard for you to understand—"

"No, it isn't." Ben offered a quick smile. "Anyone with eyes can tell you two are closer than sisters." He took another sip of coffee and reflected on the situation. "Alright," he caved in, "you can stay, but from this point forward we all stay together. You, Julie, me, Jim, Jill...we're one team."

"Agreed." Bethany nodded.

"Agreed." Julie sealed the deal.

"Well, maybe not," a voice spoke. Bethany spotted Jill wearing a brown shawl over her shoulders. "I've got bad news. Jim is running a high temperature. Poor man felt rough before bed. He's bed-bound for today." Jill touched her own forehead. "Truth is, this old turkey isn't feeling so well herself. I guess the joke is on me."

Bethany hurried over to Jill and felt the woman's forehead. "My, you are hot. Julie, get Jill to bed. I'll go make some soup—"

"I already made a pot of chicken noddle soup and a plate of peanut butter and jelly sandwiches...gave me and Jim some aspirin...rubbed some Vicks Vapor rub on Jim's chest...got some elderberry juice and zinc down us along with some orange juice. About to go slice potatoes and put them in our socks and lie down." Jill reached out and touched Bethany's hand. "You and Julie will have to watch over the place for us, Bethany. I trust you."

"Of course. We'll watch over your home as if it were our home. I promise, Jill." Bethany felt Jill's forehead again. "You're very hot. Come on, off to bed." She took Jill's hand. "Julie, stay here with Ben. I'll be back in a few minutes."

Julie watched Bethany help Jill back inside with a loving hand. "Your friend is special," Ben spoke up.

"Yes, Bethany has a very special heart," Julie agreed. "My dear friend is unique. I'm very blessed to have her in my life."

"And Bethany is very blessed to have you in her life," Ben

pointed out. "You two are a team. One isn't complete without the other. At least that's how I see it."

Julie walked her eyes over a handsome face that glowed with honest intentions and truthful desires. Ben was a decent chap—nothing more, nothing less. A decent chap. Julie wondered why a man like Ben hadn't remarried? Surely there were available women in Hay Lake or Dove Falls who would be happy to marry a nice man like Ben. One thing was certain...Julie couldn't allow herself to become emotionally involved with Ben. Julie lived in Snow Falls and Ben lived in Hay Lake—two different worlds. "It's silly standing out in the open like this. A bit dangerous, to be honest."

"I think Bethany is right, Julie. Whoever the man at the hospital was last night, he's not out to kill just yet. I think Richard Banks was the intended target for the time being. That is a mystery I can't figure out. Guess I'm Columbo, huh?"

"Oh, he's that funny chap who always has a cigar in his hand, right?" Julie asked.

"Yeah, that's the guy." Ben managed a quick smile.

"Bethany watches him, and she watches a television show called *Murder, She Wrote,*" Julie added. "I know those television shows are aired as reruns now."

"The oldies are the best shows," Ben told Julie sincerely. "At times, my aunt and I will sit down and watch old reruns of *The Andy Griffith Show*. But let me warn you, she won't watch episodes without Barney in them. My aunt has a theory that Andy Griffith betrayed Don Knotts and got him off the show because Don Knotts was becoming the real star. Who else could play the character of Barney Fife the way Don Knotts did?"

"Barney Fife...the skinny, silly deputy who carries one bullet, right?" Julie asked.

"That's the guy."

Julie wasn't too familiar with American television shows.

"Have you ever watched *Mr. Bean*? It's a British comedy show."

"Are you kidding? I love Mr. Bean!" Ben let out a jolly laugh that warmed Julie's heart. "Mr. Bean is one of my all-time heroes—better than Superman. I was never much for all the cape-wearing phonies. I mean, some guy running around dressed up as a bat...not exactly the guy running on a full engine of steam. Mr. Bean, on the other hand...well, he's awesome."

"A cop who doesn't like Superman or Batman? Goodness, wouldn't that be considered anti-American?" Julie teased.

"Maybe, but I don't think I'll waste my time and money over a bunch of guys who wear capes. Also"—a curious grin appeared on Ben's face—"let's face it...if Lois Lane can't see that Clark Kent and Superman are the same guy, then she needs to hang up her typewriter. As far as Batman goes, the guy needs to get some serious help and stop living in a bat cave."

Julie giggled. "I always kind of liked...well...the Penguin."

"Really?" Ben pretended to act shocked. "Julie Walsh, what will Batman do? The poor guy will be devastated."

"Maybe." Julie giggled again. "I just can't see myself falling for a man who dresses like a bat and has a sidekick named Robin. The Penguin...well, he's cute. Not as cute as Mr. Bean."

"Mr. Bean is a stud." Ben laughed.

For the first time in a long time, Julie was actually enjoying a conversation with a man. She didn't feel uneasy. As a matter of fact, she realized that standing and talking with Ben made her feel calm and...soothed. Was the word "soothed" correct? Yes, Julie told herself, Ben soothed her nervous heart in a way she had not expected. "Maybe when I get back to Snow Falls, we can become pen pals and write letters complaining to each other about how much we despise Batman?"

"Yeah...Alaska..." Ben felt his smile fade away. "Alaska is far away from Vermont."

Julie watched Ben turn and examine a low, dark, gray sky with eyes filled with sadness. "Is anything the matter?" she asked, even though the evidence for Ben's sudden mood change was obvious.

"Sometimes I wonder why I stay in Hay Lake?" Ben spoke in a low voice. "My brother is here...my parents passed away. I have my aunt...my aunt has a life of her own. I became sheriff because it felt like the right thing to do. I wonder if I'll ever leave Hay Lake or grow old in this small town?"

"What do you want to do?" Julie stepped up next to Ben.

Ben kept his eyes on the sky. "I don't know, to be honest. I will admit that I get tired of wearing a badge. Cops aren't appreciated anymore, and the truth is, there are a lot of corrupt cops out there that make it hard for the good cops. Hay Lake isn't a thriving crime city...well, at least it wasn't. Hay Lake is a sleepy lake community, Julie. I sit and watch my badge collect dust, and that's just fine with me. But..."

"But what?" Julie asked.

Ben sighed. "There's more to life than Hay Lake, Vermont," he confessed. "Don't get me wrong, I love small towns. I could never live in a city. But sometimes, I feel drawn to leave Hay Lake and explore other places. I'm not getting any younger. I'm a man in his early forties. I guess..." Ben finally looked into Julie's beautiful face. "I'm settled down."

Julie stared into Ben's eyes. She saw a man who was lonely. But what could she do? "Maybe you can visit Snow Falls?" she suggested. "I think you would like Snow Falls. Lots of snow...very rough winters...freezing...but it's a beautiful life up there."

"I love the snow," Ben confessed, offering a faint smile. "I couldn't live without the snow." He stared into Julie's eyes, then looked away before the beautiful woman standing before him captured his heart. "But before I consider visiting Snow Falls, we have a killer to catch."

In the far distance, a man named Steven Frosellan took a sip of coffee and checked the time. Soon he would take a ride out to Jim's and Jill's land and see if Bethany Lights was still around.

By the time noon arrived, Ben was running a fever. Whatever virus was attacking Jim and Jill had dug its claws into him. "You have a high fever. Off to bed," Bethany insisted.

"Bethany, I'm fine..." Ben offered a weak argument. The truth was, he felt like a ton of bricks had fallen from the sky and smashed into his head. "We're in the middle of a murder investigation."

Julie pushed a glass of orange juice into Ben's hand. "Bed," she said sternly. "Bethany and I aren't leaving the bed and breakfast today. The doors are all locked. The alarm system is activated. It's raining again. Everyone will remain indoors."

"Julie is right." Bethany fished a bottle of aspirin out of a crowded kitchen drawer. She opened the aspirin and spilled two capsules into her left hand. "It's noon, so you can have more aspirin in four hours. Julie will bring you some chicken soup and more orange juice. Now, take this aspirin and get to bed."

Ben didn't know whether to feel loved or annoyed, but decided on the former. "Stay inside. Please," he implored, taking his aspirin from Bethany.

"We will." Bethany waited until Ben washed his aspirin down with some orange juice. "Bed. Go."

Ben glanced into Julie's eyes. Julie pointed upstairs. "If you see or hear anything—"

"We'll come and get you," Bethany promised.

"I checked the built-in generator—"

"I'm familiar with built-in generators." Bethany thought back to the lake house her mother owned in North Carolina. *Boy, am I familiar with built-in generators.* "Bed."

"Alright, alright, I'm going. But I have to call the station and let them know my situation. I'll call when I get to my room." Ben studied the kitchen with careful eyes and walked away.

"Love, you and I are bound to get sick," Julie worried.

"Honey, if it's any consolation, I rarely get sick. I was surprised when I got sick last winter." Bethany ran a quick hand across her own forehead. "I feel as cool as a snowflake. Let me check you." Julie's appearance resonated a healthy glow, but when Bethany felt the woman's forehead, a huge frown appeared. "Julie, you're burning up."

"Am I? I feel fine." Julie felt her forehead. "I do feel warm, but love, I feel fine. That's the truth."

"Honey, when I was sick last winter, you took excellent care of me. Now I'm going to take care of you." Bethany fished two more aspirin out of the aspirin bottle. "Aspirin, orange juice, bed. I'll bring everyone up a bowl of chicken soup shortly."

"But...but..." Julie didn't want to go to bed. She felt healthy as an ox. "Love, we have a killer on the loose, and you were given until tonight—"

"Julie, we're not leaving our friends. Now, bed." Bethany quickly poured Julie a glass of orange juice. "Take your aspirin."

Julie sighed, accepted her glass of orange, and reluctantly swallowed two aspirin. "I'll be on my laptop. Maybe I can get my son to talk?"

"Really?" Bethany asked carefully.

"No." Julie sighed. "My son still thinks I'm the bride of Frankenstein. My ex-husband has brain-washed him. And sadly, love, my son isn't growing into a good chap. Just the opposite, to be blunt. My heart breaks. I feel responsible."

"Don't," Bethany pleaded. "Julie, your son has to make his own decisions. I never had children, so I won't stand here and pretend to understand what you're feeling, but I know that you're not responsible. Julie, you're an incredible woman, and sometimes—as lame as this statement might sound—the skunk sprays where it wants."

"I never heard that statement before, love...but the statement matches my situation." Julie reached out and patted Bethany's arm. "I do have a slight headache. Other than that, I'm feeling well. If you feel sick, please let me know. We will work as a team to take care of each other, okay? Promise?"

"I promise." Bethany offered her best friend a loving hug and saw her off to bed. "Whew, what a morning this is turning out to be," she whispered, making a straight path back to the kitchen after walking Julie upstairs. "I'll be glad to—"

"Hello, Bethany."

Bethany froze. A strange man was perched at the kitchen table, holding a deadly gun across his lap. "How did you get in? I mean..." *Where did this man come from? How did he get inside? Impossible. The security alarm is set.* "I thought I would never see you again. The visit you paid me last night at the hospital seemed to be—"

"You're not leaving Hay Lake, are you, Bethany?" Steven asked in a low voice while keeping his head tucked low enough for a gray fedora hat to hide a pair of mysterious eyes.

"No," Bethany offered an honest answer. If she was going to die, there was no sense in playing innocent. "I won't leave my friends."

"I assumed." Steven didn't raise his head. "You're a very

stubborn woman—or should I say, y'all are sure stubborn folk."

"You—"

"Me." Steven nodded. "I think I do a nice southern accent even though I'm from southern California. I dated a woman from Woodstock, Georgia once. That woman taught me how to put cheese in my grits...before I killed her."

"What do you want?" Bethany demanded.

"The woman I killed tried to kill me first. Self-defense is never an easy action to justify." Steven slowly raised his head and revealed a strong, handsome, brilliant face. "You're wondering if I killed Richard Banks?"

"Did you?" Bethany demanded.

"Of course I did," Steven confirmed. "That's my job. I have to eliminate all threats, Bethany. Richard Banks was festering around in quite a few poisonous pools. Rhonda Banks was only aware of half of what her husband was doing." He lowered his eyes again. "I killed off a deadly snake. Nothing more, nothing less. Think of me as a monster. However, if you knew the truth, you would probably thank me."

"Are you CIA? FBI?" Bethany demanded. "I want the truth."

"Bethany, why do you persist in asking questions? I ordered you to leave...for your own safety. If you were smart, you would realize I'm acting like a friend."

"A killer."

Steven raised his eyes again. "No, Bethany." He spoke in a hard voice. "I'm not a killer. I never was, and never will be. Richard Banks had to die."

"Why?"

"Do you want the actual truth, Bethany Lights? Or do you want the watered-down version?" Steven stood up, causing Bethany to step back. "You were involved in three murder cases...kid's stuff compared to real life."

"People were killed. I don't consider murder to be children's—"

"Bethany, if I wanted you dead, you would be dead. The rookies you dealt with in the past were weak and pathetic, arrogant rats that infested a space that no longer exists for them. Can you understand that?"

"In a sense, yes. Now tell me why Richard Banks had to die."

Steven shook his head and sat back down. "Richard Banks was part of a human trafficking operation, Bethany. Richard Banks was preparing to start an illegal—if I should say it so bluntly—prostitution operation in Hay Lake." He lowered his eyes. "Those women are now free, and the monster they were being sold to is dead. Am I regretful? No. I did my job."

Bethany stood in silence. Was the mystery man sitting before her speaking the absolute truth? It seemed that the answer was yes. "I—"

"There is a lot of evil going on in this world. One less monster is no longer part of that evil."

"I understand that the world is evil." Bethany took a second to clear her mind. *Alright, Bethany, think. This guy isn't here to shake hands and walk away. Play smart...be smart...be productive.* "If Richard Banks was your target, why are you still lingering in Hay Lake? Rhonda Banks? I don't think so."

Steven slowly placed the gun he was holding into a hidden shoulder holster. "Bethany, do you believe in coincidences?"

"Yes."

Steven nodded. "Smart woman." His voice became more relaxed. "Bethany, Jill Cunningham was involved with a young man, Wayne Tyler. Does that name ring a bell? It should. Jill told you about him."

"You bugged this house."

"Of course I did." Steven folded his arms over his chest. "The last thing I expected was for two nosy women to show up. When I discovered you were involved with Sarah Garland—"

"Spencer."

"Detective Sarah Garland," Steven pressed forward, "is a brilliant woman. I'm truly impressed with her record, and even more impressed that she and her friend Amanda Hardcastle killed the Back Alley Killer. The Back Alley Killer was a man on my list I could never track down. No one is perfect, I guess, but that's beside the point. My point is, Bethany, that I want no unneeded headaches. Wayne Tyler is loose, and my sources believe he's heading in this direction. When he arrives, I'll kill him and leave."

"You threatened to kill Jill."

"I played a little rough hoping that Jim Cunningham would force you and Julie Walsh to leave," Steven admitted. "Jim is a tough old alley cat. He stood his ground. I respect that. I'm not a monster."

"Who are you? CIA?"

"No." Steven shook his head. "I once worked for the CIA. Now I work for a different agency that has become a thorn in the side of the CIA, the FBI, and the White House. I suppose you can say I'm part of the cleanup crew. My job is to dispose of the trash."

"Wayne Tyler is trash?"

"Wayne Tyler was taken from prison by the FBI and brainwashed," Steven spilled a few beans onto the floor. "Ever hear of a false flag, Bethany?" Bethany nodded yes. "All the shootings you hear about on the news are planned...well, not every single shooting, but the shootings the media drools over and gives hours of airtime to, those are the ones to watch. You see, the FBI finds themselves a sap—a real loser, if you will—and offers that person a job. Don't ask for details because no details will be provided. All I will say is that the FBI primes that person to become a puppet that will carry out a task to push a corrupt political agenda forward."

"I'm aware that we live in an ugly time."

Steven nodded. "Wayne Tyler is a killer, Bethany. He killed ten people in Los Angeles and escaped from the FBI. The guy is much smarter than people believe...and he's also someone carrying a big chip on his shoulder."

"Jim and Jill?"

"Blames them for his arrest." Steven nodded. "No matter. I'll be waiting for him. That's why I don't need you here snooping around. You have the truth now, so leave."

"My friends are sick. I can't leave," Bethany confessed. *Do I leave now? Is this man speaking the truth? My gut is telling me yes. Are Jim and Jill in any real danger? My gut is telling me no.* "I'll leave when my friends are better. You have my word."

Steven studied Bethany's face. "My target could show up at any time, Bethany. My sources anticipate my target's arrival will be sometime tomorrow, but it's always safe to ride a wave of caution. With that said, I suggest you take Julie Walsh and leave. Sheriff Nayes can go back to his home and let his aunt take care of him. Jim and Jill Cunningham can take care of each other. No harm will come to them. You have my word. I'm only after rats, Bethany. Jim and Jill Cunningham are good people."

"Who are you?" Bethany asked in a voice that sounded desperate more than demanding.

"Bethany, who I am isn't important. What I do is." Steven slowly stood up. "I'm a man about your age, Bethany. I spent too much of my life working for the wrong people, making the wrong choices. Now I'm atoning for my mistakes. I'm trying to make America a safe place. There's a lot of trash out there." To Bethany's shock, a deep and painful expression gripped Steven's face. "I was once a fool. Now I see the truth. Maybe someday before I die, atonement will be made."

Steven walked toward the back door. "Wait!" Bethany couldn't explain it, but something about the mysterious man immediately captured her heart. "I...don't know what to say or really think. This case surprised me. I assumed I was dealing with—"

"An everyday killer?" Steven asked. "No, Bethany, you're dealing with me." He reached into the side pocket of the trench coat he was wearing and pulled out a small black device. He held up the device, pressed a green glowing button, and waited. A few seconds later, a red glowing alarm pad sitting beside the back door clocked green. "Take Julie Walsh and leave Hay Lake, Bethany. Go back to Snow Falls and forget you ever saw me. If you tell anyone about me...well, what will anyone do? Chase a shadow?" He pulled open the back door. "You have the truth, Bethany. Leave."

Bethany moved toward the back door but stopped. She watched Steven fade away into a hard falling rain with miserably confused eyes. *Yes. I have the truth...whoever you are...but my gut is telling me there is more to the truth than you're letting on. I can't leave, I won't leave, until Julie and I know the entire truth. There's more going on here than meets the eye.* She walked over to the back door, looked out into a cold gray rain, spotted only shadows, and closed the back door. *I need to call Sarah, but how? This house is bugged. There has to be a way. Maybe if I'm smart, I can use that truth to my advantage and outwit my opponent. If I'm smart...if I'm stupid, I might get myself killed. What a twist this story has taken.*

chapter ten

Bethany sat at a lonely kitchen table until night arrived. During the hours in between, she checked on her friends, ran hot chicken noodle soup up and down a flight of steep stairs, checked temperatures, refilled tissue boxes, and issued aspirin. By the time night arrived, she was exhausted from playing nurse. "I'll sit here and have a quiet cup of coffee." *I haven't been able to call Sarah, but I texted her and informed her of the situation. I don't think there's any hidden cameras around. All I can do is wait.* A cell phone sitting next to a brown coffee cup buzzed rather than let out a loud ring. Bethany quickly snatched it up. *Sarah replied to my messages...let's see what information she has for me…wait, this text is from Conrad.*

Text message from Conrad Spencer:

Bethany, there is a shadow organization called D.R.I.P., Department of Repairing Internal Pain (strange name, I know). D.R.I.P. is considered a terrorist organization by the FBI, CIA, Department of Homeland Security, and other alphabet soup agencies that waste taxpayers' money. D.R.I.P goes around killing off a lot of bad people. The organization is composed of rogue agents from different countries. An insider claimed each agent works for D.R.I.P. as an act to reconcile past wrongs...an atonement. I couldn't get any names, but Peter is still hard at work. He'll come up with more than I could. As far as we can tell, D.R.I.P. actually does good work and gets rid of a lot of dirty rats. I'm not saying I condone the organization, but in my professional opinion, I would say back down and leave Vermont. You're in way over your head against highly trained professional killers. If you were given a slot to leave, take it and go. You're family, Bethany, and I don't want to see any harm come to you. Sarah is on the horn with Peter worried sick. There's nothing we can do to protect you. Please take Julie and come home. If Sarah knew I was writing this text, she would get very mad at me. I'm writing this because our backs are up against a high wall. Please come home.

Bethany lowered her cell phone with an uncertain hand. *Well, that's it. If Conrad thinks I should throw in the towel, then there's nothing I can do. I want the truth, and I feel there's more going on here than meets the eye, but what else can I do? I've been warned three times by a man who could have easily killed me. Perhaps I should be wise and stop kicking sand in the face of a growling dog.* She bit down on her lower lip and began to respond to Conrad's text when a hard hand struck the back door. Bethany jumped, nearly dropping her cell phone and knocking over a cup of hot coffee. "Who...who is it?"

No one answered.

Bethany quickly bent down and snatched the gun Jim had given her out of an ankle holster. "Who is it?" Bethany hollered, standing up on scared legs.

No one answered.

Bethany glanced over her shoulder. No one was standing in the kitchen doorway. Fearful chills ran down her back. *What do I do? Run upstairs and get Ben? Open the door? Stand exactly where I am? What if there's a killer outside trying to lure me out? The rain has stopped, the skies are dark, the land is muddy, though would the man who works for D.R.I.P. dare return? Would he risk leaving his tracks in the mud?* She stood still as a million questions raced through her mind. "Who is at the back door? Answer me!"

No one answered.

The alarm pad was glowing red. No one was trying to disarm the alarm. *I have to be smart.* Bethany snatched up her cell phone and called Ben, even though he was right upstairs. "Someone hit the back door. Get down here. Hurry."

Ben didn't have to be told twice. He jumped out of bed—even though he was sicker than a dog—threw on a pair of boots, grabbed his gun, and raced down to the kitchen.

"I'm sorry to bother you, but I heard someone hit the back door," Bethany explained, looking at a fever-consumed man running into the kitchen with his gun at the ready.

Bethany knew the kitchen was bugged. She had reluctantly kept her encounter with the mysterious man a secret from everyone. Silence, it appeared, was the best weapon at the moment...at least until a feasible plan could be developed.

"Alright." Ben nodded at Bethany, who had her gun ready for action. "Cover me. I'm going to open the back door...might have been a night bird. Sometimes a night bird will fly into a door or a window." He checked his gun and nodded at the back door. "If you see me shoot, be prepared to do the same."

"Alright." Bethany tensed up. No night bird or stray animal had struck the back door. The hand of a living, breathing human had hit it. "I have your back, Ben."

Ben felt like cow flop. Every inch of his body ached. His nose was stuffy. His throat was sore. He was suffering from a fever. The life of a law man was never an easy one. "Okay, here we go...stand back and give yourself room." He eased to the back door on silent legs, studied a red glowing alarm pad, and entered a code that Jim had given him. The alarm pad clicked from red to green. Ben nodded, used his left hand to disengage a heavy deadbolt lock, and cautiously eased the back door open.

Usually, a storm door would have to also be bypassed, but Jim didn't see fit to attach a storm door to the back door. The back door was made of heavy solid wood and firmly weatherized. Storm doors, Jim complained, caused more trouble than they were worth, just another door to open and close. Ben was grateful he had to open only one door. But when he looked down and saw what was waiting on the ground, his heart dropped.

A dead body was lying at the bottom of a set of back porch steps—lying face down in mud. All Ben saw at first was a shadow lying on the ground, but instinct spoke the loudest in dire situations. Ben quickly reached his hand back into the kitchen and flipped on a porch light. "Rhonda Banks!"

"Rhonda Banks!" Bethany rushed to Ben's side and looked outside. And there, lying face down in mud, was the dead body of Rhonda Banks. "Oh my..."

Ben quickly scanned the darkness but didn't see anyone or anything. "What in the world is going on here?" he asked Bethany.

"I don't know." *I honestly don't know. Did the mysterious visitor just leave me a deadly message? Or...is Wayne Tyler out in the dark?* She spun back around. "I know you can hear me! Was this your doing? Did you kill Rhonda Banks? If you didn't, then you need to come back to the bed and breakfast!"

"Who are you talking to?" Ben demanded.

"Do you hear me?" Bethany continued to scream from the kitchen. "Rhonda Banks is dead! Did you kill her? If not, then maybe Wayne Tyler did? I don't know. If you're trying to help, then help me! I'm not going anywhere until you do! Do you hear me?"

"Bethany?" Ben grabbed Bethany's arm with a firm but gentle hand. "Who are you—"

Bethany dropped her head. "Ben, you will hate me...probably arrest me and never trust me again. I have something important to tell you. But first, we have to do something about the body. We can't leave that woman lying in the mud."

Julie came bursting into the kitchen before Ben could respond. Jim and Jill appeared right behind her, wearing matching brown robes. Both were armed and ready for war. "What's going on?" Jill hollered through a sore throat.

"Rhonda Banks is dead. Someone left her body at the bottom of the back steps," Ben explained.

Jim ran to the back door in a pair of old slippers and looked over Ben's shoulder. "Yep, that's Rhonda Banks all right," he confirmed, and backed up toward his wife. "Ben, any idea what's going on? Any idea why someone would leave Rhonda's body in my backyard?"

"Maybe Bethany knows?" Ben nodded at Bethany.

"Love?" Julie asked through a stuffy nose. She hugged a warm, blue robe and stared at Julie. "What's going on?"

Bethany dropped her head. "The man who escaped from the hospital last night was here...in the kitchen. He appeared after I walked you upstairs, Julie."

"What? How?" Ben demanded.

"How did anyone get past the alarm?" Jill asked. Her head was hurting so bad, she couldn't even blink. What a horrible night.

"I wanted to tell everyone, but I had my reasons for remaining silent." Bethany went for her cell phone. "I sent Sarah a message and asked her to help me. Conrad sent me a message right before I heard someone hit the back door. This is what Conrad wrote me. Read silently—the kitchen is bugged." Bethany handed her phone to Ben, who skimmed Conrad's message with confused eyes and passed the phone to Julie. She read Conrad's message, glanced at Bethany with scared eyes, and handed the phone off to Jim and Jill. They read Conrad's message together, and simply stared at Bethany, waiting for answers.

"You have all read Conrad's message," Bethany said. "Now, let me tell you what was told to me today."

She glanced at the back door and shook her head. *Rhonda Banks is dead. How? Who tracked her down? The man who works for D.R.I.P.? Wayne Tyler? Someone else? I don't know. What I know is that it's time to get a grip on the mystery man and bring him out into the open.*

She drew in a deep breath and spoke in a careful tone. Uncertain words slipped from her mouth and landed on four sets of listening ears. "That's what was told to me," Bethany finished, hoping that whoever the mystery man was had heard every single word she spoke. "Now you can make sense of Conrad's message. Conrad ordered me to throw in the towel, take Julie, and return to Snow Falls. I was considering that option when someone hit the back door."

Jim reached out his right hand and rubbed an aching neck. "Why would someone leave Rhonda's body in my backyard? It makes little sense. The man you spoke to, Bethany, it seems like he's trying to clean up a mess."

"Wayne Tyler..." Jill's voice entered the air distressed and nearly defeated. "So Wayne blamed me...I always felt he did. I tried to help him...I tried to change him..." She stumbled over to the kitchen table and sat down. "Jim, I need a glass of cold water."

"Sure thing, honey." Jim hurried to pour his upset wife a glass of cold well water. "Here you go."

Jill accepted the water and looked at Bethany. "You're a smart woman, Bethany, and I know you had your reasons for keeping your lips sealed. I can see that you knew nothing could have been accomplished even if you had told us. So tell me, what do we do now?"

Bethany locked her eyes on the front door. "Ben is going to have to create a crime scene and have the body of Rhonda Banks taken away. Whoever killed Rhonda Banks will surely watch."

"I better get on the horn." Ben dashed over to the kitchen telephone and made a call. "This is Ben. We have a dead body at the Cunningham place. I need every available man on the scene. Call Fred...well, wake him up, Mae. Fred is the county coroner. I don't care if Fred is sick—I'm sick, too." His voice became hard and professional. "We have two dead bodies. I don't want the body count to rise. Do as you're told, Mae. Is that clear? Good. Tell Fred I want this situation silent. I don't want panic in Hay Lake...good…no, I'll call the mayor."

Julie walked over to Bethany, took her hand, and gently pulled the exhausted woman over to the side. "Love, we need to call Sarah. I think we're in over our heads."

"Me, too," Bethany admitted. "But Julie, right now I need time to think. I can't put my finger on it, but the man who appeared at the hospital and inside this kitchen...I don't think he's bad. Yes, he admitted to killing Richard Banks, but after he told me what Richard Banks was planning to do…well, I certainly don't condone murder, but maybe certain people are better off dead?"

"What about Rhonda Banks? I thought Rhonda Banks told you she was planning to leave America?" Julie asked.

"Someone obviously got to Rhonda Banks before she could leave the county, honey. The question is who?" *Yes, the question is who. My gut is telling me the mystery man didn't kill Rhonda Banks. Wayne Tyler? Possibly, but how does Wayne Tyler connect to Rhonda Banks? How does some loose marble Jill used to foster tie into the death of a woman who was obviously eager to leave America?* She rubbed the bridge of her nose with a tired hand. "Question marks are lethal friends."

"I agree with that statement, love." Julie patted Bethany's arm. "You've had a rough day. You need to rest. I'll take over downstairs for a bit."

"Honey, you're sick. I'm not." Bethany felt Julie's forehead. "Your fever is down a little, but you're still warm."

"Well, I admit I feel rough, love." Julie scanned the tense

kitchen. Jill and Jim looked awful, consumed with worry and confusion. Ben met Julie's eyes, shook his head, and made a call to the local mayor. "Love, the next time we leave Snow Falls, let's go to a deserted island in the middle of nowhere."

"The snowman would follow us to the island, honey. The snowman will follow us anywhere." Bethany drew in a deep breath, walked to the back door, and looked down at the dead body lying face-down in a bit of mud. "Where did your life get you?" Bethany whispered to Rhonda Banks's corpse as a hard gust of icy night wind growled past her face. "Where did being so evil get you? Nowhere."

chapter eleven

Steven waited until a flashing ambulance drove away from a tense farmhouse that had been transformed into a cozy bed and breakfast. To his relief, Ben Nayes, the local sheriff, followed the ambulance, leaving Bethany Lights and Julie Walsh alone with Jim and Jill Cunningham. Steven had no idea who had delivered the dead body of Rhonda Banks to Bethany Lights. Wayne Tyler had been captured hours before by a brave State Patrol. A deadly shootout had occurred, and the State Patrol put a bullet in Wayne Tyler's right shoulder and left leg. A second State Trooper who had arrived on the scene put two bullets into Wayne Tyler's stomach. Wayne Tyler was lying on an operating table in critical condition. So who killed Rhonda Banks? That was the question of the hour —a question Steven had to find an answer to.

After Ben drove away, tailing the ambulance like a tick searching for a dog, Steven cautiously waited, hiding in the loft of an old barn. Using a pair of night vision goggles, he surveyed a dark and damp land. The land appeared clear, but Steven was a trained soldier. He spent an hour in the loft and dedicated a second hour to patrolling the outskirts of the land, roaming through dark woods and examining lazy cow pastures attached to rolling hills. When a hard rain fell,

Steven concluded that the land was clean...or was it? Someone had delivered a dead body to Bethany Lights. The unknown killer had to be lurking about, but Steven couldn't locate anyone or anything except a few deer and a grumpy raccoon. "The land is secure, yes, but I know better."

Steven used every caution in his bag of tricks as he approached Jim's and Jill's house. He quickly disarmed the security system and slipped through the back door. Bethany, Julie, Jim, and Jill were still standing in the kitchen. Steven didn't act surprised. He knew that a welcome party was waiting for him. "Starting to rain," he spoke in a clear voice, closing the back door with a firm hand. "Mind if I have a cup of coffee?"

"Want a donut?" Jim asked, blowing his nose into a handkerchief.

"Please...and thank you," Steven nodded. Bethany studied Steven's hard face, prepared the man a cup of coffee, and retrieved a coffee donut off a plate sitting on the kitchen counter. She took both items to the kitchen table. Steven accepted his gifts, sat down, and removed his hat, revealing a tough military style haircut. "I don't know who killed Rhonda Banks. Wayne Tyler was pulled over by a state trooper a few hours ago and decided he would rather die than be taken into custody. A shootout took place. Wayne Tyler is now lying across an operating table in critical condition with several bullets in him. I'm sure his face will be spread across the morning newspaper."

"So it's true. Wayne Tyler was on his way to Hay Lake to kill me and Jim." Jill's voice dripping with fear. "I always knew deep down that Wayne was criminally insane. I didn't want to admit the truth, I wanted to believe against all hope there was a chance for him."

"You care about mangy mutts, honey, there's no crime in that." Jim patted his wife's arm. "I wanted to believe that there was good in Wayne, too."

"Not as much as I did." Jill shook her head and turned her attention to Steven. "Who are you?"

"My name isn't important—"

"I want a name," Jill demanded. "Give me a fake name, but I swear if you don't give me a name, I will take a broom and chase you out of my home."

"Alright. You can call me...Steven." Steven disclosed his real name, assuming the four people staring at him would think it was a fake. He took a sip of coffee and focused on a donut sitting on a saucer. "Rhonda Banks was supposed to be in London by now. I have no information on her death. That's the truth."

"I believe you." Bethany took a seat across from Steven. "I received some information about you today. A text. I know who you work for."

"D.R.I.P.," Steven confirmed, and then took a bite of his donut. "I'm a rogue CIA agent working to make right for all my wrongs. It's that simple. I will not sit here and pretend I'm a saint because I'm not. I've killed innocent people. For that, there are no words. My life is now dedicated to getting rid of the trash. Enough said."

"Alright then." Jim nodded. "We accept your words and believe you are telling the truth. I have one question: are you on our side?"

"I'm here to find out who killed Rhonda Banks. Until I do, yes, I'm on your side. Once my mission is complete, I'll leave and you will never see me again. Simple. Direct."

Julie focused on Bethany, who was staring at Steven with deep, thoughtful eyes. "Love?" she asked, speaking through a stuffy nose.

"Whoever killed Rhonda Banks left her body for me to find. I need to know why," Bethany told Steven. "Why was the body of Rhonda Banks brought back to this land?"

"I don't know," Steven said honestly.

"Rhonda Banks was shot twice in the chest. She had dried

blood attached to her clothes. The woman wasn't killed on this property," Bethany continued, keeping her voice stern. "Any ideas?"

"No."

"Alright then." Bethany retrieved her cell phone and called Sarah. "Sarah, a man named Steven is sitting before me. He claims he doesn't know who killed Rhonda Banks. The floor is yours."

Far away in Snow Falls, Sarah quickly took a sip of hot coffee as Conrad leaned back in a kitchen chair and waited. "The man you're speaking to is named Steven Frosellan. Mr. Frosellan worked for the CIA as a hitman. His assignment was to kill political opposition. Eleven years ago, Mr. Frosellan became a rogue agent. Ever since then, he has been marked for death by the global government. Isn't that right, Mr. Frosellan?"

Steven simply took a sip of coffee. "You're a resourceful woman, Mrs. Garland—sorry, Mrs. Spencer. Your friend Peter is also very resourceful. I'm impressed." He glanced at Bethany. "This is why I attempted to scare you away. Now that the cat is out of the bag, so to speak, perhaps we can work as a team?"

"Mr. Frosellan, what do you know about Rhonda Banks?" Sarah stepped back in. She paused for a second, studied a wooden back door that was holding back a vicious wind, and looked at Conrad, who folded his arms and nodded. "Rhonda Banks is dead. We need to be honest with one another."

Steven took a sip of coffee. "Detective—"

"I'm retired," Sarah informed Steven. "My husband, Detective Spencer, is standing in the kitchen with me. If you want to speak to an active detective, you can speak to him."

"Detective Spencer has an impressive reputation, Sarah," Steven spoke, allowing his voice to become personal. "Your husband is the type of man I wouldn't mind having at my side. I'm sure the feeling isn't mutual. My record is stained with blood. I'm now marked as a filthy rat."

"That's not true," Conrad spoke up. "You've taken out a lot of bad people, Steven. Yeah, you killed many innocent people...I studied your records. You joined the Marine Core at seventeen and became a sniper. At the age of twenty, the CIA recruited you. You came from a hard family. Your mother ended up in prison for drugs when you were eight and left you to be raised by your stepfather who ended up in prison for nearly beating you to death. You were tossed about from one foster home to the next...ended up in juvenile hall for getting into countless fights—you stabbed a man, robbed a store. The Marine Corps barely accepted you. A soft-hearted judge fought on your side. By the time the CIA got its claws in you, you were ripe."

"I suppose I was," Steven agreed, showing no concern that Conrad had brought up personal matters of his past. His sudden change in attitude caught Bethany off guard. "I was a furious young man. I saw the world as my enemy. I wanted to be on the winning team. Becoming a CIA agent made me feel invincible. I was finally on top of the world, in absolute control of everyone. Only...I was on the losing team, and I wasn't in control. Too bad it took many so long to learn the truth."

"What changed you?" Bethany asked before she could catch herself. "What made you risk your life and turn against the CIA?"

Steven lowered his eyes. "I killed a man campaigning for a certain politician. I placed myself in the man's home and waited for him to return. Unbeknownst to me, the man had picked up his daughter for weekend custody. When this man entered his home, I attacked him with fierce force. My agenda was to subdue him and implant what we called at the CIA 'heart-stopping juice' into his blood stream and toss his body into a bathtub filled with water." His voice filled with pain.

"When I attacked, I heard the most awful scream...'Leave my daddy alone!' The man's daughter, an eight-year-old little girl, hit me. I looked down into a terrified face and realized I had become a monster that would haunt the dreams of an innocent girl. I...at that moment, something happened. I burst out of the man's house and ran...and ran...and ran."

"What happened?" Julie stepped forward. "Where did you run?"

Jim and Jill both urged Steven to continue. "You're among friends now," Jim assured Steven.

Steven kept his eyes bowed. Friends? What were friends? He didn't trust anyone, not even the people he connected to the shadow organization he worked for. Betrayal was the number-one killer among friends. "The man I intended to kill was a youth pastor campaigning for a politician threatening to unravel a sensitive agenda that could have destroyed many careers. The politician in question was preparing to reveal a corrupt budget plan if elected as senator. At the current time, this politician was a state governor—don't ask who because the man is now dead, but not at my hands." He raised his eyes. "I was prepared to kill an innocent man because I was ordered to. No questions asked—strike, kill, vanish. At least, until I looked down into a pair of eyes that sent fire through a cold, dead soul. It was at that moment I realized I had become a true monster."

"We can all change." To everyone's shock, Jim approached Steven and touched the man's shoulder. "We all do things we regret, but in the end, we can change. I had a buddy who did things in Vietnam—drugs...drinking...he ended up firing blindly into a hut and killed an entire family. My buddy tried to kill himself. He then dedicated his life to helping Vietnamese orphans."

Steven locked onto a pair of sincere, honest eyes that held no betrayal or deceit. Jim Cunningham was an honest man. "Well, Jim, I still have a long road before me. I may work for an organization that tries to right wrongs, but the organization I work for has been infiltrated by a lot of deadly snakes. A man doesn't know who he can trust. Therefore, I trust no one."

Trust no one...the hospital...Steven was there...Ben was watching the parking lot...trust no one...Sarah and Peter discovered Steven's true identity...Steven didn't act upset or shocked...he even confessed a personal page from his past. As a matter of fact, maybe Steven has realized a deep, horrible secret that he's been expecting. I think I might know what that secret is. "You're being set up. This is all about you, isn't it?" Bethany suddenly asked Steven.

"Possible," Steven allowed. "At first, I wasn't certain. But now that Sarah Garland—Spencer—and her friend Peter have my personal data, I'm suspecting that a target has been placed on my back. Someone is out to destroy me. My time has come. My personal data has been destroyed. The only way Sarah and her friend could have found me is if someone leaked my data from dead files...and trust me, Bethany, that task alone would require a team of brilliant minds."

"Wayne Tyler?" Bethany asked.

Steven shook his head. "Wayne Tyler's objective seemed legitimate. Now I'm suspecting maybe Wayne Tyler was going to tell me something that he wasn't supposed to know. Up until this moment, I couldn't be certain. I had to give Sarah time to help me secure a correct path to approach."

"What can we do to help?" Conrad spoke up.

"There's nothing you can do. If my suspicions are correct, all I can do is run and keep running." Steven stood up. "If I'm wrong...I don't know. Rhonda Banks is dead. She was shot twice in the chest. That type of killing is a signature kill."

"Where are you going?" Bethany asked Steven. *Why am I so worried about this man? He's a killer...well, he was a killer. His safety should not be my concern. But I'm worried about him. There's something in his eyes...a desperate cry for absolution an redemption. I don't see a monster. I see a broken man.*

"Your lives are in danger. We need to leave this place."

"Come to Snow Falls," Sarah ordered. "Conrad and I can help you."

The sound of an approaching car caused Steven to yank out a hidden gun. "That's Ben's old car," Jim said. "Ben followed the ambulance out. He's coming back now."

Steven lowered his gun and studied the situation. Was it time to run? Could he trust the people standing before him? And what about Bethany Lights? Why was Steven drawn to Bethany? What was it about the beautiful woman that captured a tortured heart? "I can't run. There's nowhere to run. The only way I'll ever be safe is if I die."

Bethany stared into Steven's eyes. *The snowman is out there. The snowman wants Steven dead because if Steven dies...we all die. Somehow, Steven is keeping us all alive, and the snowman knows it. But what can anyone do? We're trapped in a snowstorm with no way out, and when this storm ends, we might all be dead.*

Far away, a man named Tony Ricci stepped out of a hotel room and entered a wet parking lot. "Your time is short, Steven. Before I kill you, the body count will rise...starting with Bethany Lights."

chapter twelve

Ben eyed Steven with deep suspicion. "You killed Richard Banks. You openly admit that you killed Richard Banks. That's cold-blooded murder."

"Depends on the eye of the beholder," Steven replied.

Ben reached his hand down toward his service gun. Steven snatched a deadly gun free from a hidden shoulder holster before the sheriff could complete his act. Ben froze, and Steven aimed his gun directly at Ben's chest.

"Shoot me," Ben dared, offering a brave tone. There was no way Ben Nayes would turn yellow in front of Julie. A man either lived brave or died a coward.

"No." Steven dropped his gun down onto the kitchen table and held up both of his hands. "Arrest me, Sheriff Nayes. I killed Richard Banks...but remember why."

Ben met Steven's eyes—the eyes of a man who had, outside the laws of justice, killed Richard Banks. The question was, did Steven commit murder, or end the life of a rat preparing to torture innocent women? How many women were now free because of Steven Frosellan? How many women had been returned back to their husbands, children, parents. How many women would not endure years of abuse at the hands of soulless monsters? Did Steven Frosellan deserve to be thrown into a pair of handcuffs and hauled away to a cold jail cell?

"No," Ben whispered to himself, removing his hand from his black utility belt. "Mr. Frosellan, I'm not going to arrest you. You may have killed Richard Banks, but I think I might have jumped the gun by stating your actions were cold-blooded. For that, I'm sorry."

"Why?" Steven asked. "In your eyes, I'm a killer. I won't pretend to be anything other than I am, Sheriff Nayes. I have the blood of many innocent men on my hands. My hands are stained. I deserve to be put to death."

"Have you asked for forgiveness?" Bethany asked.

"I already have," Steven confessed. "Why do you think I'm trying to atone for my crimes?"

"But not in the right way," Bethany pointed out, allowing her voice to soften. *Why in the world do I care for this strange man? My own life seems to be a great mess, and to make matters worse, the snowman that once haunted Sarah is now after me. I shouldn't care one way or the other about Steven Frosellan. Yet...I can't deny that I do.* "Mr. Frosellan, there are other ways to atone."

"There is no other way, Bethany." Steven stood up and glanced around the kitchen. Julie, Jill, and Jim were standing in silence, staring at him. "I would leave, but I fear if I do, you might all die. It's not safe to stay here. Whoever left the body left a message for me. I'm certain of that now."

"What do we do, Steven?" Jim asked, sniffling into a handkerchief. "Jill and I are sick. We're not able to travel. But we will if needed."

"That's right." Jill took her husband's hand. "Jim and I spent many years of our life on the road telling lame duck jokes, Steven. We're now old and worn down and settled into a new life. Sure, we still have our sense of humor—"

Jill froze.

"What is it?" Jim asked in a concerned voice.

"Sense of humor…that's it, Jim!" Jill rushed over to Steven and grabbed his hands. "We're all present, all the players needed in the game: the sheriff, the guest, the killer...perfect! Oh, what a gag this is going to be! One last laugh on all the bad guys!"

Steven looked into Jill's eyes, his expression curious. "What's the plan, Mrs. Cunningham?"

"Call me, Jill, darling." Jill let go of Steven's hands. "Listen, everyone, here's the plan." She ran to Jim. "We're going to fake the biggest murder scene in the history of Hay Lake! Ben, you're going to make the scene look authentic...and you"—Jill pointed directly at Steven—"you're going to die!"

"Ah, the murder mystery scheme you and I were trying to bring to life." Jim grinned. "Jill, you're brilliant." Jim planted a warm kiss on his wife's right cheek. "Alright, honey, what's the plan?"

"Steven kills us all and Ben plays the hero—he kills Steven." Jill pointed at Ben. "Ben, you're going to have to make the murder scene look real. Can you do that?"

A wide grin touched Ben's sick eyes. "Jill, you can count on me!"

"After we fool the bad guys"—Jill focused her attention back on Steven—"get your backside to Snow Falls, Alaska and stay there." She swung around to Bethany and Julie. "Call Sarah and tell her the plan. Sarah is going to make it look like you're dead."

"Got it." Bethany quickly nodded. "Julie and Steven, are you on board with this plan?"

"I'm on board, love," Julie told Bethany.

Steven stood very silent as his mind contemplated every single possibility. Would Jill's plan deceive the snakes that wanted him dead? To Steven's astonishment, he realized that Jill's plan actually held a great volume of possibility. "Jill." Steven walked over to the sick woman and took her hand. "If this plan of yours works, I will cook you a pot of my special chili."

Bethany watched an excited grin appear on a face usually set in cold stone. *Steven believes in Jill's plan...and so do I. My goodness, Hay Lake is full of twists and turns. What a vacation this has turned out to be. Instead of trying to find the killer who shot Richard Banks, we're trying to save the killer from other killers. Life is full of sharp pieces of glass.* "Alright, Jill, let's get to work."

Jill agreed. "Jim, take Julie and get all the fake blood we have in the basement. Ben, take Steven up to the attic. There's a box of bloody sheets and fake body parts. I need the bloody sheets. There's also a box of fake guns, knives, and so on. We'll need them. Bethany, go into the family room. You'll find some old filming equipment Jim and I were going to use to make a homemade commercial. Bring the equipment out to the barn." She quickly blew a runny nose into a handkerchief. "We all might catch our deaths making this movie, but the barn is the final scene. Now, chop chop, everybody get to work!" She clapped her hands excitedly.

"Wait a minute," Ben ordered. He carefully turned his attention to Steven. "Listen, I don't know you and you don't know me...so what I'm about to say, you can disregard."

"Alright. Speak your piece." Steven prepared to be kicked into the dirt.

Ben took a few seconds to clear his thoughts. "Mr. Frosellan, every man has a chance to redeem himself. What you did in your past—who you were—is dead. I can see a great deal of regret and pain in your eyes. It's clear to everyone standing in this living room that you're trying to redeem yourself. I'm going to do everything in my power to help you, and I want you to know..." he extended his right hand to the other man. "You have a friend in me. I'm not much—just a small-town sheriff—but I'm extending my hand."

Steven lowered a pair of cautious eyes and studied Ben's

hand. In his past, it would have taken a pair of hungry grizzly bears ripping him apart to even consider shaking a man's hand. Now, as Steven stared into Ben's eyes, he felt his right hand lift into the air. "And you have a friend in me, Ben," he said candidly, shaking the sheriff's hand.

Ben smiled. "Then let's get to the attic and find those bloody sheets."

"Lead the way."

Bethany watched Ben and Steven rush out of the kitchen. "Let's go." Jim took Julie's hand and ran her to a closed door standing beside the refrigerator. "Basement, here we come!"

Jill waited until Jim dragged Julie down into a finished basement before turning to Bethany. "Call Sarah."

"I'm on it." Bethany quickly called Sarah on her cell phone. "Sarah, we have a plan."

"Let's hear it." Sarah grabbed Conrad's arm. "Bethany has a plan."

"Well, Jill came up with the plan. Here's the plan." Bethany drew in a deep breath and carefully confessed Jill's plan in precise detail. "My question is, can we kill a man like Steven Frosellan and bring him back to life in Snow Falls?"

Sarah paced around a brightly lit kitchen. "It's possible...if Ben does his job right, and if I do my job right."

"What do you mean?" Bethany asked. *Sarah's mind is bubbling. She's hatching a plan of her own. I should count my blessings I have such a friend. There is no way I could have ever figured out, much less survived, this case on my own.*

"I'm going to come to Hay Lake and transport two dead bodies back to Snow Falls for burial," Sarah explained. "Steven Frosellan will be a third body—a hidden body—and Peter will have to assist me."

"Sarah, can this really work?" Bethany asked, feeling a tinge of hope—if not excitement—enter her fearful heart.

"Bethany, if there's one thing I've learned during my life, every chance a person takes will either succeed or fail. But don't worry, we have Amanda on our side...and I think my crazy friend might come in handy."

"Amanda? How?" Bethany asked.

"Wait and see." Sarah smiled. It felt good to be back in the saddle again, even if the ride was short. "Sit tight, Bethany. I need to call Amanda and then have a meeting with my dear husband who is looking at me like I've gone insane."

"You are insane." Conrad sighed and rolled his eyes. "I better call Andrew. I have a feeling we're going to need his help on this."

"We sure are." Sarah nodded. "In order to save our friends, we're going to need a network of support. Bethany...handle matters on your end."

"Do you really have confidence in me, Sarah?" Bethany asked, feeling a sudden surge of enthusiasm. "I think I dropped the ball on this case. As a matter of fact, every murder case I've become trapped in has been a miserable experience. I survived each case by the skin on my nose. I'm not as smart as you would like to believe."

Sarah felt it was time to carry out some serious damage-control tactics. "Bethany, when I became a cop, I was green as grass. I can't count the times I nearly got myself killed or someone else killed. By the time Pete met me, I wasn't prepared to chase down killers. Pete taught me everything I know, even though Pete claims I learned a few things on my own. My point is that—" Before Sarah could finish, Amanda burst through the back door, soaked with snow.

"Okay, where's the fire? I'm ready for action! Conrad, go get me a grenade launcher! Sarah, get me a flame thrower! We're going to Hay Lake, Vermont to save our girls! I've already called the airport and reserved our plane tickets!"

Conrad rolled his eyes. "The abominable snowman covered in snow and wearing an oversized blue coat and hat that was fifty percent off at O'Mally's. I'm sure the enemy is terrified."

"Watch it, you smart-mouth bloke!" Amanda marched over to Conrad and slugged his right arm. "Go make me a cup of coffee! Sarah and I have some planning to do! The girls are back in action!"

Sarah fought back a grin. Amanda was insane—but oh, how Sarah loved her Amanda. "Bethany?"

"I heard, I heard." Bethany smiled. "Tell Amanda thanks, and that I love her."

"I will. And listen, if I didn't believe in you, I wouldn't have suggested you fly to Vermont." With those words, Sarah ended the call, leaving Bethany on her own again.

"Well?" Jill asked.

Bethany put down her cell phone. "I better go get the filming equipment. We have a lot of work to do. But..." She paused, her eyes locking on the back door. Suddenly out of nowhere—as if an icy hand punched her in the gut—a strange feeling washed over Bethany's heart. *What if there is a second killer?* a deep inner voice asked. *What if the people who want Steven dead didn't kill Rhonda Banks? What if...*

"What is it?" Jill asked.

Bethany walked over to the back door and ran a bare hand across a sea of rough wood. "Jill, a thought just occurred to me. If the body of Rhonda Banks was left at the back door, how can we be so sure the woman was actually killed by the people who want Steven dead?"

"Who else could have killed that awful spider?" Jill asked.

Bethany stopped rubbing the back door and slowly turned to face Jill. "It seems as if we have all of our pickles in a barrel, so to speak. But now I'm wondering if maybe we need to search for one last pickle?"

A heavy moan left Jill's mouth. "Bethany, I love you deeply, girl, but you're making my mind hurt. I can only deal with so much." She walked over to Bethany and put a firm arm around the woman. "Like my daddy used to say, adventure down one path at a time and see where that path leads to. Okay?"

"I understand." Bethany promised. "I'll get the filming equipment."

Bethany left the kitchen carrying a heavy question mark over her head. When she reached the staircase, Steven was waiting for her. "Steven?"

"I sent Ben upstairs." Steven nodded for Bethany to move closer. Bethany obeyed. "Have you figured it out?"

"A second killer?" Bethany asked.

Steven shrugged his shoulders. "I can't be certain. Rhonda Banks seemed to have been killed by a professional. However—"

"Your gut is nagging you?"

"Badly," Steven confessed. "We may believe we're seeing what's behind the curtain...and maybe we are. But there could be a hidden trap door. The only question is, who is hiding under the trap door?"

"Maybe we will find out?"

Steven frowned. "For the first time in my life, Bethany, I don't know who is hiding in the shadows. But maybe you do?"

Outside in the rain, a hidden killer was waiting.

chapter thirteen

Blood. Terror. Horror. Murder. The scene was set.

Bethany stationed herself beside a damp bale of hay. "Alright, everyone, I think we're ready. Jill, what do we do?" She had to speak over a loud, pouring rain. She drew a deep breath of air that smelled of hay, dirt, rain, and fallen autumn leaves. *Autumn is supposed to be a beautiful time of the year. So far, autumn hasn't exhausted its beauty in ways that soothe the heart. I'm preparing to allow myself to be killed, though I prefer yellow autumn leaves over the sight of blood.*

"Steven, you're the expert. So here's the deal." Jill hugged a heavy green coat as she spoke. "You're going to kill everyone and I'm going to film it. While you kill everyone, talk into the camera. Talk to some unseen enemy you're going to search down and kill. After you kill everyone, kill me...and when you do..." She turned to Ben. "Ben, you bust out of nowhere. Make sure you appear before the camera and shoot Steve dead, and then call for help as if the world is ending. Got it?"

"I understand." Ben glanced around the dark barn lit only with a few dim flashlights placed on old hay bales. The space felt like an actual horror set. "Julie, how are you feeling?" he asked, worried.

Julie hugged a blue coat and let out a miserable sneeze. "Horrible, love," she confessed.

"Me too," Ben agreed. "Uh...maybe someday, if we ever go on a proper date, we can skip the horror movies?"

"Maybe..." Julie sneezed again. The air was damp and freezing. Not exactly the perfect atmosphere for a woman running a fever. "We need to hurry. Please. I'm sick...and I also have the creeps."

"I agree with Julie." Jim hurried to check a stack of blood-stained sheets lying over a stack of hay bales. "We're set, Jill. Let's get the movie rolling before we all catch our deaths out here."

"Steven, got your gun?" Jill asked, speaking over the rain just loud enough to be heard.

Steven held up a realistic-looking fake gun loaded with blanks. "I'm impressed with you and Jim. You two were prepared to operate a murder mystery bed and breakfast with all the works."

"Be impressed later. Julie, step in front of the camera. Jim, when I give you the signal, turn on the camera."

Jim placed himself behind an old-fashioned movie camera covered in dust. He checked the camera with skilled hands and nodded. "The camera and filming equipment are ready...the flashlights are set about just right...we're ready for action."

"Alright." Jill hurried over to Julie. "When Steven shoots you, I'm going to press this button." She held up a wire attached to what appeared to be a black box. "The special effects toys we have won't hurt you, but you will feel a small punch when I activate the blood pouch I attached to you, honey. There is going to be a small explosion, so you have to make it seem like you're being shot and hit the ground hard. Can you do that?"

"I can, love," Julie promised, staring into a desperate face filled with shadows.

"Bethany." Jill moved on to Bethany. "Steven is going to do a one-two punch. He's going to kill Julie and then plow into you. The scene will be quick. Can you handle it?"

"I can," Bethany promised.

Jill spun around to Jim. "When Bethany gets shot, you run out in front of the camera screaming your head off. Steven will kill you...fall onto Bethany and Julie."

"Got it." Jim nodded. Oh, how he loved his wife—and how he loved it when his wife took control of an act. Jill was great on stage, demanding and appealing at the same time.

Jill turned to Steven. "When you kill Jim, I will freak out. Start ordering me to calm down and...so on and so on. Convince the audience that you're in control. Eventually, you kill me because I refuse to calm down, and that's when Ben shows up and kills you. Ben, Steven will kill me off-camera because I have to control the blood pouches attached to everyone and make sure they explode right on cue."

"Remind me to never make you mad, Jill," Ben tried to joke.

"There's nothing to this," Jill insisted. "Me and Jim have been studying up on special effects and all that. It's all silly stuff...hopefully, the silly stuff we're about to play with will save our lives. Now, everyone get—"

Before Jill could finish her words, a shadow burst through a pair of open barn doors. "Hold it!" Phil Goshen hollered. "Don't anybody move!"

Bethany remained very calm, quickly grabbed Julie's hand, and glanced over at Steven, who nodded. So Bethany had been right about who the hidden killer was—a last-minute wild guess had turned out to be a stroke of genius.

"Phil Goshen...what on earth?" Jill exclaimed.

"Shut up!" Phil hollered.

Bethany watched a sixty-two-year-old man wearing a black coat use his right foot to kick one of the barn doors closed. "It ends, do you hear me!" Phil hollered, sounding more like a mad cow than a threatening killer. "The game ends!"

"What game?" Steven asked.

"You know what game, Mr. Frosellan...but if you play your cards right, I might tell you what I did to Tony Ricci." Phil aimed a deadly gun directly at Jill. "I don't want to kill anyone, but I have to. Everything is in order."

"Tony Ricci?" Steven narrowed his eyes. "Mr. Goshen, I'm afraid you've been played."

"I know that," Phil hissed. "At least, I've allowed Tony Ricci to think he played me. Tony believes he has been in control ever since you arrived in town, Mr. Frosellan. When Tony informed me you were in town to kill Richard Banks, I saw many doors open...even a door to kill Rhonda Banks."

"You and Rhonda Banks were an item, right?" Bethany spoke up. "That's how you killed her. You were the person she was texting the night I visited her at the hospital, right?"

"You're a smart woman, Ms. Lights...too smart." Phil moved his gun away from Jill and aimed it at Bethany. "Tony told me all about you. My job is to kill Jill and Jim Cunningham...Tony is going to blame your deaths on Mr. Frosellan...turn Mr. Frosellan into a media star, so to speak. Tony and I were preparing to strike tomorrow night after the heat about Rhonda's death died down. Our plan was to scare you and your friend off. Tony assumed Mr. Frosellan would remain behind. He didn't tell me why."

"Mr. Goshen, you've been played by a clever man," Steven growled. "You're not outsmarting anyone."

"Oh, but I am." Phil grinned. "Tony Ricci is at his hotel room…dead. I shot him. You see, Mr. Frosellan, I'm a clever man. If you play your cards right, you and I can work as a team. Tony Ricci told me you are skilled at laundering dirty money. Is that correct?"

"No." Steven shook his head, scanning the dark barn. There was no way in the world a little runt like Phil Goshen had killed a trained killer like Tony Ricci. Tony Ricci was the only man alive who could give Steven a run for his money. "It's like I said...you were played."

"I seriously doubt that." Phil swung his gun toward Steven. "You can live or die, Mr. Frosellan. If a man like Tony Ricci hated you with so much venom, maybe you're the kind of man I want on my team? The choice is yours."

As Phil spoke, Jim eased his hand into the front right pocket of his coat. It was time to end the game all right, but not in the way Phil Goshen was hoping. No one aimed a gun at Jim's wife and got away with it. "Tony Ricci isn't dead." Steven kept Phil's attention drawn away from Jim.

Jill wasn't interested in Tony Ricci. She wanted to know how Bethany had figured out a complicated riddle. "Bethany, how in the world did you know Phil Goshen was involved?"

Bethany nodded at Ben and Julie. "When Ben and Julie informed me that the bank president had thrown a lot of loose information at them, I thought little of it at first. After all, Julie is a beautiful woman. Maybe Julie offered a flirty eye that caused a weasel to loosen his tongue...or maybe not?" Bethany focused on Phil. "The word 'loans' kept ringing out in my mind. Ben told me you knew Richard Banks was allowing many unqualified business loans. One unqualified loan should have been enough for you to take serious action, right? But what if you and Rhonda Banks were setting Richard up for failure?"

"You're too smart—"

"When I visited Rhonda Banks in the hospital, she was wearing a pink robe. Rhonda was taken to the hospital in an ambulance...so who brought her the robe? Could have been anyone, right? When I entered the hospital room, Rhonda Banks was holding a cell phone she quickly hid from me. Why?"

"Bethany, I'm not following," Jill confessed as Jim continued to reach for a hidden gun.

"Well, I suppose Rhonda Banks could have been talking to anyone. But what sealed my theory about Phil Goshen is that Ben told me Richard Banks's bank files were placed under a lock and key. Why? A man in your position, Mr. Goshen, would want to help the police. You tossed a few bits of information at Ben, right? Or maybe you were setting Rhonda Banks up for the kill?"

"Oh...I see..." Jill could barely believe her ears. "A real life *Murder, She Wrote*. Right, Jim?" Jim nodded. "Bethany, you are one smart cookie, but why didn't you tell Ben? He could have arrested this rat!"

"Because Richard Banks was killed," Bethany confessed. "If Richard Banks was killed, that means the man was connected to Steven, which means Steven is connected to people who want him dead. Surely," she insisted, "Phil Goshen had to somehow be connected to the network, assuming I was right about him."

"And you were," Steven told Bethany as he stared at Phil Goshen with eyes that turned vicious. There was a time to show mercy and a time to strike. Steven was preparing to strike down a worthless snake without mercy.

"Let him live."

"What?" Bethany's words caused Steven's attention to leave Phil Goshen and look over into a pleading face.

"Let him live, Steven. There's been enough killing," Bethany begged. *Steven is preparing to kill Phil Goshen. I can read the tone of his voice. Two people are dead. We don't need anyone else to die.* "Ben—"

"Don't anyone move...I have the gun...the first person who moves dies!" Phil hollered. "Are you all insane? You're acting as if I'm not in control. You're all dead...starting with you." For whatever reason, Phil pointed his gun directly at Julie. "Prepare to die!"

Before Phil could carry out his threat against Julie, a single gunshot rang out. All Bethany saw was Phil Goshen's body fly backward and crash into the closed barn door. Bethany swung around and threw her eyes at Jim. Jim yanked a hidden gun out of his coat pocket and yelled: "It wasn't me!"

"It was me," Ben spoke in a regretful voice, lowering his service gun. "I killed Mr. Goshen." Ben walked over to Phil's body, bent down, and checked the man for any signs of life. "He's dead...I killed him." Ben bowed his head. "Never killed a man in my life. He was going to shoot Julie."

Steven ignored Ben. "Everyone get inside the house. Hurry!" he demanded. "Tony Ricci isn't dead! He'll kill us all...in my past, I could stand toe to toe with Tony Ricci. Not anymore."

Bethany didn't question Steven. She grabbed Julie's hand and ran for the open barn door. "We'll continue our movie later!" Jill cried out. "Let's get moving while we still can, Jim!" Jim grabbed his wife and ran. As he did, a shadowy figure appeared in the open barn door, raised a hard foot, and kicked Bethany so hard in her stomach that the poor woman was flung backward and sent crashing into Jim and Jill, knocking them down.

Ben rolled off to his side and tried to get a clear shot at the intruder. Tony Ricci put a bullet in Ben before he could blink an eye—and then placed a bullet through Steven's shoulder before the man could get a clear shot at him. Steven stumbled back and struck a pile of hay bales.

Julie cried out in horror and ran to Ben. "No..."

Tony Ricci stepped into the barn, keeping his gun aimed at Ben. "Nice set-up you have here, Steven. I liked the idea of faking your death. But as you can see, the movie has been canceled."

Bethany raised her eyes and look up into a face that, to her horror, hissed and growled with the purest form of evil she had ever seen in her life. *The snowman...the snowman has taken form in that monster's face. That's what the snowman looks like.*

"Steven, Steven, Steven..." Tony shook his head at Steven.

"Did you think I wouldn't find you? Did you think you could hide inside of D.R.I.P. forever? Oh, you hid for a while, but Dan turned back to the...dark side?" Tony flashed a hideous grin. "We're both *Star Wars* fans, right, Steven?"

"No," Steven growled, holding his left hand over a bleeding shoulder. "I only liked R2-D2...never cared much for Darth Vader. Guy had a breathing problem."

"See, now you're insulting my hero!" Tony threw a hard, black combat boot down onto Bethany's chest and aimed the gun he was holding at her. "We're going to have a talk, Steven...if you tell me where the money is located, I'll vanish and let your girlfriend live. If you refuse, all of you will die a slow and painful death. Is that clear?"

"No!" Julie cried over Ben's body while allowing her hands to feel his chest. Ben was wearing a protective vest. Yes, the man was unconscious, but he was alive. "He's dead! You killed him...he's not breathing!"

"Shut up and keep your hands where I can see them!" Tony roared at Julie. "Steven, shall we talk? I don't have all night!"

Something in Julie's voice told Bethany that Ben was still alive. *Ben is our only hope now...I hope we stay alive long enough for Ben to save us.* Bethany looked up at Tony Ricci again. An evil snowman grinned down at her.

It was time to die.

chapter fourteen

Steven refused to show any pain. Tony had sent a fierce, hungry bullet through his right shoulder. The bullet had torn through and dislodged out of the back of his shoulder, leaving a bloody mess behind. No matter. Steven was a tough guy. He knew how to handle pain—and he had trained his left hand to be as deadly as his right hand. He needed to buy time to gain some momentum. Tony Ricci would die. "Are you going rogue, Tony?" he asked.

"Let's just say that maybe it's time for me to leave the scene, Steven. The game has become too complicated for my taste. A hungry little rat had a talk with me about you—I knew my retirement fund had appeared." Tony kept his boot pressed down against Bethany's chest. "Look, Steven, we can let the past lie. Understand?"

"You killed Laney," Steven growled.

A sickening grin flashed across Tony's cruel, soulless face. "You and I were close at one time, Steven. Laney loved us both—"

"Laney loved me!" Steven narrowed his eyes. A deep wave of pain crashed down onto an agonizing wound that had never healed. "You'll kill me before I tell you where the money is."

"See, that's not the answer I want!" Tony aimed the gun he was holding back down at Bethany. "Steven, I'm not a sentimental guy. I play the game, and I play it well. Laney was personal...I admit that. But who cares? The woman is dead. It's time to move on. Now," Tony's voice transformed into the voice of a deranged prison guard who took joy in torturing innocent men, "it's like this...you're going to tell me where the money is, or you will watch me kill everyone in this barn one by—"

"Kill them! What's it to me, Tony? Huh?" Steven snapped. "You forget I play the game well, too. Do you really think I'm concerned about any of these people?"

"Don't play me, Steven. You have a conscience."

"Maybe I turned to D.R.I.P. to make people believe what I wanted them to believe. Maybe I'm still hungering to kill Wallace Mayberry? Did that ever occur to you?" Steven asked.

Tony grew silent. "Wallace Mayberry is untouchable, and you know it."

"We'll see." Steven checked the palm of his left hand. He was bleeding pretty bad, but so what? "Kill whoever you want—kill me—but you're not getting the money. You have my word."

Tony's face drooped in defeat before quickly transitioning toward anger. When Steven gave his word, that was it—the end, no more life to the story. What was Tony to do? How was Tony going to force Steven to tell him where millions and millions of dollars of stolen money was hidden? Was Steven hungering to kill Wallace Mayberry? Was the man's stint with D.R.I.P. simply a coverup? "Fine, I'll kill this woman and we'll see if you have a conscience or not."

"Wait!" Jill cried out. "Please, whoever you are...why?"

"Why?" Tony let out a diseased laugh. "You're nothing but a weak animal, lady...a worthless bottom feeder that needs to die. Right, Steven? Only the strong survive. Isn't that how the game works?"

"Shut up and kill them already...and then it'll be just you and me, Tony. Maybe after you kill everyone"—Steven held up his left hand and formed a hard fist—"we can go a few rounds man to man, huh? Unless you're too much of a coward."

Ben's eyes fluttered as Steven danced around a deadly boxing ring with Tony. He heard someone crying above him. What was going on...why did his chest feel like it was on fire? Why was it so hard to breathe. "Play dead," Julie whispered in Ben's ear, pretending to be sobbing silently over the dead man. "Please, play dead."

Julie's thick British accent entered Ben's heart rather than his ears. He lay still and listened. Tony had a clear view of his captives. Bethany, Jill, and Jim were lying right in front of him. Ben and Julie were off to the left a few feet. Steven was directly in front of the killer. If anyone moved an inch, Tony would shoot them down like dogs. The only advantage Ben had was that the wounded man was lying on his stomach rather than his back.

"I beat you once, remember, Tony?" Steven asked, keeping his voice hard and daring. "I beat you into a bloody pulp. I would have killed you then, but your friend showed up with some serious fire power."

"You were lucky."

"How's your nose?" Steven cut through Tony's words with a sharp knife. "I liked the sound of your nose breaking, Tony. Did it hurt?"

"Don't press me, Steven."

"You're not getting the money!" Steven roared. "Do what you will do and get it over with. You know me, Tony. I don't turn coward. I've sat through many torture sessions. You can't do nothing to me Wallace Mayberry hasn't already done." He checked his shoulder again. "You know how bad Wallace

Mayberry tortures people, Tony—you sat through one of his torture sessions."

"Yeah, I did." Tony gritted his teeth. He wanted Wallace Mayberry dead more than he wanted Steven dead. But Wallace Mayberry was untouchable—for the time being.

"Steven—"

"Shut up!" Steven yelled. "Tony, you're stupid! Do you think Wallace Mayberry doesn't know where you are...where I am? You led him right to us! I'm surprised a strike team hasn't burst into this barn and gunned us all down by now. But trust me, a strike team will be on scene any minute."

"Impossible!" Tony roared back at Steven. "No one knows where I am. I'm invisible!"

"Sure you are," Steven struggled to create a plan in his mind. Tony had the high ground. One wrong move, and the next bullet Tony fired would go through Steven's head. Tony Ricci was a deadly shot—accurate and lightning-fast. "You're stupid, Tony! Why do you think I'm standing here running my mouth? It's only a matter of minutes before we're all dead anyway."

"Don't try and bluff me—"

"Your friend there"—Steven nodded down at the dead body of Phil Goshen—"is the bait, Tony. Do you believe Phil Goshen—"

"I controlled every step that rat took," Tony snapped.

"Sure you did—and so did I." Suddenly, a plan whispered into Steven's mind. "I don't go down without a fight, Tony. You know me better than anyone...look..." He reached his left hand into the pocket of the trench coat he was wearing. "Don't shoot. I'm not going for my gun..."

Tony prepared to gun Steven down. But if he did, the stolen money would never be seen. He watched with extreme caution as Steven slowly reached into a deep pocket and pulled out what appeared to be a black device with a red blinking light on it. "What is that?"

"Your demise," Steven answered. "When Phil Goshen showed up, I activated the GTAD...the Global Tracking Agent Device, Tony. You know what they are. When the device is activated, the intelligence satellite goes on alert. I never got rid of my little toy. If I'm going down, then I will make sure all the dynamite I planted explodes."

"No!" Tony let out a loud, angry cry and looked around the shadowy barn as if a million hidden lions were preparing to pounce on him. "You—"

"Committed suicide?" Steven asked. "Yeah, I did. When Phil Goshen mentioned your name, I made sure you would die along with me. I'm just playing you for the rat you are and buying time, Tony. By now, Wallace Mayberry has a strike team in the air."

Bethany lay on a cold, damp floor staring up at Tony Ricci with eyes filled with uncertainty. *Is Steven telling the truth? Is he bluffing a killer? I don't know. All I know is that the snowman is present...in Tony Ricci. And now, the snowman is panicked.* "Let us go...please," Bethany struggled to speak.

"Let the women go," Jim demanded. "What kind of a man kills a woman?"

"A coward," Steven answered for Jim. "Tony Ricci has no problems killing women, do you, Tony?" Steven tossed the black box he was holding down at his feet. "We're all dead, Jim. It's only a matter of minutes now before we hear the strike helicopters arrive. There's nowhere to run."

"No!" Tony threw his eyes at Steven, breathing like a madman. Steven had called in a pack of deadly wolves. Tony knew he had seconds—if that—to escape. But without the money? Tony was now marked as a rogue agent, and that was a title of death. He could run, but where to? Steven was his golden ticket. "I'm going to kill you—"

"So kill me already. You'll be doing me a favor, Tony. When the strike team arrives, I will not be killed. Wallace Mayberry will want to have words with me…and you...the hard way." He placed his left hand back onto his wounded shoulder. "Kill me already."

Tony knew Steven was right. Any death he offered his enemy would be merciful. Leaving Steven alive would allow true torture to crawl onto the scene. "You think you won...you think you've outsmarted me, Steven? You didn't. I'll find the money. One way or the other."

"Good luck." Steven tossed an ugly grin at Tony. "You'll never find the money, Tony. All you're going to do is spend the rest of your life running...running and looking at every shadow you pass. Fear is an interesting friend to carry with you, isn't it?"

"Julie, my gun," Ben whispered as Steven and Tony continued in a war of words. "Shoot him..."

Julie closed her eyes. Did she have the courage to take Ben's gun and kill Tony? "Play dead." Julie moved her right hand toward Ben's gun while crying. Tony was momentarily too occupied with Steven to see her, but Steven immediately noticed Julie's movement. "Kill us off, Tony, and run. You know it only takes a matter of minutes to get a strike force into the air."

Tony stared at Steven through eyes dripping with lava. "I would kill you, Steven...but I won't. I will let Wallace Mayberry deal with you. But to make sure you don't run…" Tony aimed his gun at Steven's legs. "I wonder how painful it feels to have your kneecaps shot out. Huh, Steven?"

Bethany knew Tony was preparing to cripple Steven. She threw up her hands and grabbed a muddy boot and tried to throw Tony off balance. Tony pressed his boot down even harder. "Get...away..." Bethany coughed.

"Shut up!" Tony growled, lowering his eyes down onto a scared face. Did Steven once love Laney Andrews? Maybe. Bethany Lights didn't resemble Laney Andrews in any way, yet there was something about the woman that was striking...mysterious...appealing. Tony wondered—a sick and demented type of curiosity—if he should leave Bethany alive and take the woman with him? "Maybe I'll leave you alive, huh?" he asked, believing he had a matter of seconds to escape.

"I don't think so!" Bethany tried to throw Tony's boot off her chest again.

Tony lifted his boot and planted it down against the poor woman's throat. "You're going with me...we'll have lots of fun..." He lifted his eyes and focused on Steven. Bethany knew the man would cripple Steven and then kill everyone...including Julie. But what could she do? The snowman had the higher ground.

Steven kept watch on Julie out of the corner of his eye. If Tony was going to gun his legs out from under him, so be it. "Wait!" Jill cried. "Please...why?"

"Shut up!" Tony roared.

"Hey, don't you talk to my wife like that, you slug!" Jim roared back. "You're nothing but a punk, do you hear me? A pathetic punk—a coward with a gun—nothing else! Do you hear me!" Jim formed his hands into two fists. "Put that gun down and face me like a man, punk...or are you too scared, huh?" Jim knew he was painting a target on his chest, but Steven was up to something. Jim felt it, and so did Jill. Whatever Steven's plan was, the man needed help.

"I think Jim could take you, Tony." Steven let out a taunting laugh. "What do you say? Are you brave enough to go ten rounds with an old Marine?"

Tony looked down at Jim's face. Jim Cunningham represented everything he despised about mankind—goodness, decency, morality, integrity, and true courage. A courage Tony knew he would never possess. "You're a dead man."

Bullets erupted into the air, causing the inside of the barn to sound as if a barrage of artillery rounds had exploded. The bullets tore into Tony's face like hungry, venomous snakes latching onto a shadowy closet monster. Bethany looked up just in time to see an evil snowman cry out in pain and then vanish, allowing a monstrous face to appear...but a face that was now-human. *The snowman...I saw him leave...*

Tony Ricci didn't know what hit him. He was dead before his body hit the floor of the barn.

"Not bad," Steven spoke in a calm voice and walked over to Julie and squatted down. "You did good."

Julie was in too much shock to lower Ben's gun. Had she just killed a man? Yes. "I...well..."

Bethany scrambled to her feet and ran to Julie. "Honey, are you all right?" she begged, taking Julie into her arms.

"Hot dog, that's what I'm talking about!" Jill grabbed Jim and stood up. "Julie, lunch is on me!" Jill and Jim hurried to Ben and checked on the man. "Ben, speak to me!" Jill slapped the sheriff's face a few times.

"I'm alive...I'm alive," Ben promised, mumbling out pained words.

"Yeah, you're alive." Jill wiped cold sweat off her forehead. "For a minute, I thought you were dead."

"Me, too." Jim patted Ben's shoulder and looked at Steven. "Nice bluff."

"I try." Steven let out a worried sigh. "But..." He surveyed the barn. "Tony Ricci was running this operation. We need to finish the movie when Ben is able. We have to make the outside world believe I'm dead...but there's going to be a few changes made to our movie."

Bethany looked up into Steven's shadowy face as she held Julie in her arms. *I think the snowman attacked because it knew Steven joined us and tried to stop it. The snowman will be back. It'll never go away. Never.*

Outside in the dark night, a cold, hard rain continued to fall.

chapter fifteen

"Peter has assured me that your plan worked," Sarah said confidently as she sipped on a cup of coffee. "Sheriff Ben Nayes went on national television and made a public statement. Jill and Jim were at his side. Also," she added, "I was filmed at the airport Montpelier with Amanda, watching two empty caskets being loaded onto an airplane."

"It's hard to cry on demand," Amanda complained, shoving a chocolate donut into her mouth. "You Yanks expect so much drama."

Julie smiled a forced smile, but a smile nonetheless. Amanda was a nut. "Can I have a donut, love?"

"No, all mine." Amanda grabbed a box of delicious donuts and held them to her chest. "Get your own. I'm in a grumpy mood. Sarah won't let me have no more kosher chili dogs."

Sarah folded her arms over a green sweater with a red leaf sewn on the front. "Amanda, you've nearly eaten every kosher hot dog in O'Mally's. Can we save some for the customers?"

Bethany grinned. *I'm home where I belong. Back in Snow Falls, back at O'Mally's. I don't think I'll ever leave home again.* "I watched the news," she told Sarah, grateful to be wearing a green sweater that matched her friend's. It felt wonderful to be back at O'Mally's helping her family prepare for a major autumn sale. All autumn clothes would be marked at half off. Thanksgiving was on the horizon, but in Snow Falls, winter arrived early—and so did the snow. "I have to admit that Ben did a great job. If I didn't know any better, I would say the entire scene looked very authentic."

"Me too," Julie agreed, giving Amanda the stink eye. "Can I have one donut? Just one?"

"Well...just one..." Amanda reluctantly released the box of donuts she was holding and scratched at herself. "These sweaters are so itchy and silly. Green sweaters with a red leaf...you Yanks have no taste, love!"

"We need to match, and you picked the autumn sweaters we wore last year, remember?" Sarah reminded Amanda. "Yellow sweaters with a muffin on them...not exactly stylish."

Amanda winced some. "Well, I wasn't feeling well."

"You were feeling fine." Sarah laughed, then glanced around the cramped office. "Alright, we have to open the doors in half an hour, but before we do..." She focused directly on Julie, watching the brave woman take a coffee donut from the box she was holding. "How are you doing, Julie?"

Julie met Sarah's eyes. It was clear as day that Sarah loved Julie more deeply than a sister. "I'm still a little shaken up. I had a nightmare last night. I saw myself shooting that awful man repeatedly. Sometimes I jump at my shadow."

Bethany placed a loving arm around Julie. "You saved our lives. Tony Ricci was preparing to kill us."

"I know." Julie looked down at the donut she was holding. "Bethany, Sarah, Amanda...can I tell you something? And you all might think I'm insane for what I'm about to say, but I need to say it or go mad."

"We're right here, honey. We love you. You can tell us anything," Sarah assured Julie.

Julie reached out and handed Amanda the donut she was holding. "When I shot Tony Ricci," she began, speaking in a low, scared voice, "I thought I saw...oh, never mind. You'll call the mental institution on me and have a bunch of men wearing white coats chase me with a butterfly net."

"No, we won't," Amanda promised. "Look, I'm crazy and no one cares." She shoved the donut Julie had relinquished into her mouth. "I don't care if people think I'm crazy. All I care about is getting my hands on more kosher chili dogs."

"Amanda," Sarah sighed. "Julie, honey, we love you. You can tell us what's in your heart."

Bethany stared into Julie's eyes. She understood. *Julie saw the snowman, just like I saw the snowman.* "Did you see the snowman?" she asked.

Julie's eyes grew wide. "Yes, love. I did...did you?"

Bethany nodded. "I saw the snowman leave Tony Ricci when you shot him."

Sarah stiffened. An image of a leather-jacket-wearing snowman chewing on a candy cane entered her heart. "So the snowman is still alive," she whispered.

"Yes," Bethany confirmed, looking to Sarah's pale face. "Sarah, the snowman is after me and Julie now because it can't defeat you and Amanda. I don't know how I know this, and it took me three murder cases to finally understand it." She stood up from a wooden chair sitting in front of the office desk. "When I arrived in Snow Falls, I faced killers. I was thrown into a state of confusion and shock that consumed every fiber of my being. I arrived in Snow Falls a broken woman...a woman who wrote that perfect murder, remember?"

"We remember." Sarah nodded. "Bethany, your book wasn't—"

"My book was a way to vent, right?" Bethany asked miserably. "But maybe I truly killed my husband in my book, Sarah, in my heart? Maybe I allowed myself to actually kill him in here." She touched her heart. "Maybe that's why the snowman is after me now...because I understand the darkness. And Julie." She looked at her dearest and best friend. "Julie understands the darkness, too. I know she hasn't spoken of it, but she left London carrying a shadow."

"I believe I did, love," Julie agreed. "Now my son thinks I'm dead. My ex-husband thinks I'm dead. I allowed myself to die because I was worried our connection to Steven might harm my son. I was—and still am—afraid of the snowman."

"Me too," Amanda confessed, and then gobbled down another donut. "Julie, love, that snowman is one evil creature. I can't tell you how many times me and Los Angeles nearly kicked the bucket because of that pile of sour water." Her lovely face became very solemn. "The snowman is back...and it's not going away."

Silence filled the office. Bethany, Julie, Sarah, and Amanda all looked at each other. "I saw the snowman leave Tony Ricci's face," Julie finally whispered. "I know what I saw, and I'll never forget it." She slowly folded her arms. "Bethany is right, and I've thought about this. The snowman attacked us as soon as we arrived in Snow Falls, and it follows us."

"Which means the fight isn't over," Bethany added. "Julie, we deceived our fleshly enemies, but not the snowman. Peter got us all new social security numbers and fake names—problems that Jill didn't consider when she suggested we all die...problems none of us considered except Steven, but he didn't say a word. Anyway, we're dead to the world, and in Snow Falls, we're two new people. But the snowman knows who we are. The snowman can sense us...sense our hearts."

"I agree," Sarah spoke up. "The fight is far from over, girls. But for now, you're safe, and that's what matters."

A hand tapped on the office door. Bethany stiffened and bent down to snatch a gun out of a hidden ankle holster.

"It's Steven," Sarah said.

Bethany paused, locked her eyes on the office door, and

sighed. *So this is how it's going to be from now on. Fear is an interesting friend to carry with you.*

"Come in, Steven," Sarah called out, easing her right hand away from a desk drawer hiding a Glock 17.

Steven glanced down a short hallway and checked the arm sling his right arm was resting in. He felt vulnerable and uncertain. Was he safe? Were Bethany and Julie safe? Everyone was resting in a secured safety net, but was the thought only an illusion? "Hello," Steven spoke evenly as he opened the office door and carefully stepped into the cramped office.

Bethany saw a handsome—and mysterious—man step into the office. *Steven's eyes...he's uncertain about being in Snow Falls. He's been uneasy ever since we arrived. I can't blame him...he has many enemies.* "You're talented at breaking into buildings. The store is locked."

"Old habits," Steven confessed. "I've been walking around the back making sure no one is lurking about and checked the building for weak points. The back supply room door needs work."

"Told you, love," Amanda told Sarah proudly. "The back door couldn't keep out a sleep-walking moose."

"I know, I know." Sarah focused on Steven. "If you're standing here, that means—"

"I'm tense, yes," Steven confessed. "The scheme we carried out seems to have fooled my enemies...or so it appears. My dead body was accidentally cremated, remember? Will my enemies buy that story?"

"Ben was very convincing," Julie insisted.

"Yes, Ben was convincing." Steven nodded, but not with absolute confidence. "Wallace Mayberry won't mess with me. The truth is, Wallace Mayberry will know I pulled off a lie. The guy will go along with it...but I have other enemies."

"But isn't Wallace Mayberry—" Julie started.

"My mortal enemy? No." Steven shook his head. "In the

eyes of Tony Ricci, yes...but a man must know how to play his enemies. The truth is, Wallace Mayberry has helped me a time or two. We go way back...served in the Marines together. I saved his life four times, and Wallace never forgot. There are others who want Wallace dead, others who won't forget. I'm connected to a network of killers. That's why I've come to say goodbye. I can't stay in Snow Falls."

Goodbye? No. Steven can't leave. We've become...friends. Bethany felt a strange pain enter her heart. Why? Why was she caring for a man who could never love...a man who would always run in the shadows...a man who...who...

What? Bethany asked herself, feeling confused and hurt. *Steven isn't my husband. He's a stranger. So what if he leaves Snow Falls? That's his business, not mine...right?*

"You can leave Snow Falls, Steven, but you will never stop running. At least in Snow Falls you have friends," Sarah spoke before anyone else could.

"That's right, you silly bloke," Amanda added before wolfing down another donut. "Stop thinking about leaving Snow Falls. Don't you know all misfits belong in Snow Falls?" She asked Steven as she chomped on her donut, spreading donut crumbs all over herself.

"Amanda is right. You belong here, Steven, with us." Sarah pointed at the office door. "There is nothing out there but falling snow, Steven...and a deadly snowman is lurking in the snow. You can run, but you won't get far. And trust me when I tell you this...the snowman wants you to run. When we're separated, we're at our weakest."

A hand reached through the office door and grabbed Steven's shoulder. Steven spun around, prepared to attack. When he saw Conrad standing in the hallway, his heart dropped. "You—"

"I've been watching you." Conrad removed his hand from Steven's shoulder then shook snow off his heavy, black leather jacket and removed his black muffler hat. "Snow is going to arrive around dinner time. You better go buy some snow salt for the front walk of the cabin you're renting."

Steven stared at Conrad. How in the world had Conrad sneaked up on him? Steven was a trained killer. Conrad was a simple New York cop with clumsy feet—or was he? Maybe he was attempting to relay an important message to an uncertain man. "Conrad…"

"You're not leaving Snow Falls, Steven," Conrad told Steven sternly. "Andrew wants to see you later. Ralph is moving to Alabama to be close to his son. That means there's going to be an opening up at the station. Nathaniel Edward Dolstien. You will be the perfect person to replace Ralph."

"I agree," Sarah spoke up. "Steven, you're meant to stay in Snow Falls with us. If you accept the position at the station, you will have access to vital databases and agencies. You'll be able to keep track of your enemies."

Steven stared into Conrad's eyes—the eyes of a genuine friend—and then turned and looked into Bethany's beautiful face. Steven had no desire to leave Bethany, but he also didn't want to put the woman's life in any danger. Tony Ricci had nearly cut off everybody's lifeline. "Do I stay?" he asked Bethany, staring deep into her eyes.

"Yes," Bethany whispered, shocked at the certain tone of her voice.

"Hey, it's freezing," Ben Nayes stepped up beside Conrad. "I fixed the loose hinges on the back door...did I miss something?" He quickly removed a brown muffler cap, spotted Julie, and smiled. "Conrad and I were outside."

"I told them," Conrad informed Ben.

Ben nodded. "Steven, Conrad and I meant no disrespect. We wanted to show you that you're not safe alone."

"I must be losing my grip if two flat foots like you two can sight me in the dark without me realizing it." Steven kept his eyes locked on Bethany. Something was happening—what? Steven wasn't sure...or was he? "Okay, Conrad, tell your local police chief that I'll accept his offer. And Ben," Steven finally looked away from Bethany, "have you heard from Jill and Jim?"

"I did," Ben smiled. "Jill and Jim are going to pay us a visit at Christmas and help me get my hardware store on its legs. Jill and Jim are stars now, and Jim is running for the county seat Rhonda Banks left empty. He'll have no problem taking the seat."

"Good." Steven checked his shoulder. "Did you tell Jill that Wayne Tyler turned good in the end and that he was coming to Hay Lake to warn me? Did you tell her that the guy thought the state troopers who pulled him over were shadows instead of real badges?" Ben nodded. "Alright then..." Steven dared to look into Bethany's eyes one more time. "I need to go buy some snow salt...it snows a lot in Alaska, after all."

"I agree," Bethany told Steven as a tender smile touched her eyes. Steven smiled back and eased out of the office.

"Come on, Ben, we need to take Steven into town." Conrad slapped Ben on his shoulder. "Later, we need to go check the pipes in the cabin you bought. Your aunt keeps complaining the pipes rattle too much."

"Don't remind me," Ben moaned. "Julie, I'll see you for lunch?"

"Of course, love," Julie beamed. Ben smiled and walked away.

"See you at lunch, honey," Conrad told Sarah and moved away.

"Love you," Sarah called out.

"Not as much as I love you," Conrad called back. "Don't forget to call Mrs. Fleishman. She called me a few minutes ago. Little Conrad is out of his favorite cookies."

"Then why don't you go to the store and...oh..." Sarah rolled her eyes. "He always does that."

"He's a bloke, what do you expect?" Amanda shoved

another donut into her mouth. "Come on, Julie, we need to check the snack café before we open." She grabbed Julie's arm and dragged her out of the office.

"Amanda, wait. Uh, Julie, we open soon...will you make sure all the cash drawers are counted at an even one hundred dollars?" Sarah shot to her feet. "Amanda, we're running low on kosher hot dogs. Amanda, stay away from the snack café...Amanda!"

Bethany watched Sarah run out of the office in panic mode. *So this is my new strange life...living in Snow Falls with misfits where I belong...fighting a hideous snowman now lurking out in the darkness somewhere.* She folded her arms and drew in a deep breath. "Yes, this is my life now...and it's only beginning. The snowman isn't going anywhere...and neither am I."

Outside in an icy cold wind, a leather-jacket-wearing snowman hissed at a cozy department store soaked with early snow and vanished into a hideous song. "Oh the weather outside is frightening...so...so frightening. I'll be back, Bethany...when the snow arrives...so...so frightening..."

more from wendy

Alaska Cozy Mystery Series

Maple Hills Cozy Series

Sweetfern Harbor Cozy Series

Sweet Peach Cozy Series

Sweet Shop Cozy Series

Twin Berry Bakery Series

about wendy meadows

Wendy Meadows is a USA Today bestselling author whose stories showcase women sleuths. To date, she has published dozens of books, which include her popular Sweetfern Harbor series, Sweet Peach Bakery series, and Alaska Cozy series, to name a few. She lives in the "Granite State" with her husband, two sons, two mini pigs and a lovable Labradoodle.

Join Wendy's newsletter to stay up-to-date with new releases. As a subscriber, you'll also get BLACKVINE MANOR, the complete series, for FREE!

Join Wendy's Newsletter Here

wendymeadows.com/cozy

www.ingramcontent.com/pod-product-compliance
Ingram Content Group UK Ltd.
Pitfield, Milton Keynes, MK11 3LW, UK
UKHW021936190726
13853UKWH00004B/1471